DEAD RINGER

THE UNPRODUCED SCREENPLAY

IB MELCHIOR

Published in the USA by:
BearManor Media
PO Box 1129
Duncan, Oklahoma 73534-1129
www.bearmanormedia.com

ISBN 978-1-59393-390-6

Printed in the United States of America.
Book design by Brian Pearce | Red Jacket Press.

INTRODUCTION

This screenplay, *Dead Ringer,* an off-the-wall sci-fi yarn, was written over fifty years ago, when sci-fi script writing was in its infancy and the stories conjured up were as fanciful as possible. It was a time, when — in the aftermath of the atomic bombs dropped on Japan and the resulting radiation — the topic of atomic power and radiation was still on everyone's mind, and terms such as isotopes, neutrons, Roentgens and half-life began to enter the mainstream conversation, with everyone attempting to understand the ramifications of these terms. As such this screenplay might well be considered an almost historical contribution to movie making history.

The script you are reading is an actual copy of the script as typed these several decades ago, with only a few minor corrections, when home computers were non-existent, typewriters could not correct and white-out was unheard of. If you made a mistake you had three choices. Start a new page all over again, print the error and try to correct it by hand, or — since the old typewriter could reverse and type over what had been written — do so and simply *xxxxx* out the errors. That was the easy way, and you will see several such *xxxxx*s throughout the screenplay.

In writing the script I was intrigued with the notion of half-life, which I didn't understand at all, but I let my imagination take over and speculated that if half-life was possible, what about double-life or duplicate-life? Imagination is a wondrous thing, so I just let it run with that concept, and the result was *Dead Ringer.* The unique concept lent itself to a totally unusual and even incomprehensible conflict full of suspense and surprises, which I endeavored to convey. It was the classic sci-fi adage, that if you accept one unorthodox postulate as fact, the rest will make perfect, logical sense.

Why was the script not produced? I honestly don't remember and I can find no records in my files. All I know is, that it was about that time that I became totally absorbed with my idea and my writing of my screenplay, *Robinson Crusoe on Mars,* one of my favorite projects. Perhaps *Dead Ringer* was too avant-garde even for the most sophisticated sci-fi fans. Anyway I hope you will find your brief journey into the unpredictable world of isotopes, Roentgens and half-life of interest

Ib Melchior

DEAD RINGER

**ORIGINAL SCREENPLAY
BY
IB MELCHIOR**

The Coppage Company
3369 Canton Lane
Studio City, CA 91604
(818) 980-8806

FIRST DRAFT

DEAD RINGER

Original Screenplay
By
Ib Melchior

FADE IN

1. CLOSE SHOT. SIGN ON BUILDING

It shows the characteristic, triangular warning symbol for radiation, and reads:

DANGER!

RADIATION

2. STOCK

Over the following scene we superimpose our

MAIN TITLE

followed by the rest of the credits.

The background is a series of actual scenes taken by the Atomic Energy Commission and showing the handling of radioactive materials through the use of 'robot hands'.

It is a wholly fascinating operation. The scientists - protected by a thick lead-and-concrete shielding wall deftly manipulate a pair of metal claws with the exacting delicacy of a watchmaker. With their fingers fitted into steel tubes and rings the men cause the robot hands on the "hot" side minutely to duplicate the slightest movements of the hands and fingers of the scientists on the shielded side, while the men follow the progress of their work through a series of mirrors.

The operation we follow is that of sawing open a small radioactive metal cylinder; removing the "hot" core, and placing it in a lead container for safe removal.

The last shot of the background scene is a MED. L.S. of the laboratory area; scientists and technicians are working.

3. EXT. DAY L.S. ATOMIC PLANT. STOCK.

Over the shot appears the legend:

Karrington Atomic Research Laboratories
LOS ANGELES

4. STOCK.

A crew of men are working the intricate automatic controls and hoists moving a huge metal drum with radioactive waste materials.

5. STOCK.

Technicians are checking a lead cask for radiation with geiger counters.

6. STOCK.

A scientist is working with a fantastic looking glass tube apparatus. Radio-active liquids bubble and seethe in the complicated still.

7. STOCK.

Technicians are busy at an eight feet tall control panel; lights and meters are tracing a hectic picture of information.

8. STOCK.

Scientists are occupied at a large remote control dial panel; their work is being checked by a series of overhead mirrors.

9. EXT. DAY. MED. SHOT. MAIN ENTRANCE TO LABORATORY BUILDING.

A couple of technicians enter the building; over the door is a sign reading:

"BUILDING Q"

10 INT. DAY. MED. SHOT. DOLLY SHOT. BUILDING Q CORRIDOR.

Several doors lead off the corridor; opposite the Main Entrance the corridor forms an L, turning to the right; a couple of technicians walk down the corridor; CAMERA DOLLIES TO ONE OF THE DOORS ON the left.

11 CLOSE SHOT. DOOR.

It is a double door with two frosted glass windows; across the door appears the legend;

EXPERIMENTAL LAB D BLDG Q

AUTHORIZED PERSONNEL ONLY

12 INT. EXPERIMENTAL LAB D. MED. SHOT.

It is not a large room and every possible spot is taken up with scientific apparatus, all designed for work with radioactive materials; yet the place is not cluttered; there are several heavy lead containers, casings for 'hot' objects and isotopes; on one wall hang several pieces of protective equipment: A couple of thick lead-rubber aprons; gloves; protective goggles, etc.; one wall is taken up by a heavy lead-and-concrete shielding wall behind which are the remote controlled conveyors transporting the radioactive materials to and from the lab, the transfer table and the turntables; the 'hot' area can be observed either through lead-glass shielded window ports with thick lead shutters that can be closed over them, or by a series of overhead mirrors; at one end the shielding wall presents an opening for physical access into the 'hot' area, when there is no radioactive materials there; in front of the wall two sets of robot-hand controls hang down - looking very much like heavy dentists' drills, but ending not in drills, but in the rings and tubes, through which the operators can fit their fingers and duplicate the most delicate operation with the steel robot-hands on the 'hot'side; a complicated control panel to one side has several switches, dial wheels and push buttons.

Two men are engrossed in work; both wear white coats; one of them, DR. JAN RINDORP, a huge man, looking more like a retired wrestler than a scientist, is operating the robot-hands; the other, DR. KENNETH ROGERS, a good-looking man in his early thirties, and a top physicist, is making notations on a clipboard, and adjusting a couple of dials. There is an air of tension in the little laboratory.

KEN closes the last lead shutter over a window port and presses a button; a blinking light goes on, on the panel. He places the clipboard on the narrow table ledge before the panel.

                    KEN
              (His voice is tense)

     Shutters secure. Conveyor activated.

                    JAN
     Specimen container in place on turntable.
     Cap tongs ready.

                    KEN
     Here she comes - - -

13 STOCK

Along the remote controlled conveyor a large bottle with a dark, oily liquid moves slowly towards the laboratory transfer table.

14 INT. LAB.

                    JAN
     That's the last storage bottle left, isn't it, Ken?

                    KEN
     The last one- - -

15 STOCK

The storage bottle arrives at the transfer table; automatically it is locked in place next to the specimen bottle by the turntable.

16 INT. LAB.

Both KEN and JAN are manipulating controls and dials.

                    JAN
     Pipette ready for transfer. Fifteen cc's.

                    KEN
     Fifteen cc's . . . Check.

17   STOCK

The cap on the storage bottle is being unscrewed and removed, all by remote controlled tongs; a large pipette slowly descends into the liquid.

18   C.U. JAN.

He is tense upon his delicate work.

                          JAN
              Lowering pipette.

19   C.U. KEN

He is following the action in the mirror.

20   STOCK.

The pipette withdraws; the specimen bottle moves into place under it, and the radio-active liquid flows down into the container.

21   INT. LAB.

The men are working absorbedly.

                          JAN
              Cap going on.

                          KEN
              Ready to return storage bottle.

KEN - intent on the dials - reaches for his clipboard without looking; his hand brushes against it, and it falls to the floor with a loud clatter. JAN starts visibly; there is a small muffled thud from behind the shielding; of JAN'S hands clasped in the controls makes a desperate gesture, as he calls:

                          JAN
              Ken! The bottle!

KEN at once looks up into the mirror.

22   CLOSE SHOT. THE MIRROR.

In the mirror can be seen the storage bottle; it has fallen out of its guard ring; it is lying on its side - slowly it rolls on the conveyor, towards the edge - and the concrete floor below - - - - -

23   INT. LAB.

                          KEN
              The pipette! Jan! Use the pipette! - - -

JAN frantically manipulates his controls.

24   CLOSE SHOT.   THE MIRROR

The bottle is just about to roll off the conveyor to shatter below; from above the large pipette dips down towards it; at the last possible moment it reaches it, barely touching it, just enough to stop the roll.

25   CLOSE SHOT. JAN

His face is strained; the veins on his temples stand out.

                        JAN
            Can't reach. . . any further - - -

26   CLOSE SHOT. THE MIRROR

The bottle moves a fraction of an inch towards the edge; the pipette scrapes along its side with a faint, sharp screech; the bottle stops.

                        KEN (O.S.)
            You got it, Jan! Don't move!

27   INT. LAB.

                        JAN
            We can't...let it fall...Nineteen months
            of work - - -

KEN takes a deep breath; he looks pale.

                        KEN
            I'll have to go in there!

                        JAN
            No, Ken! Don't!

                        KEN
            You can't hold that bottle much longer. If it
            falls, all our work will be wasted.

He quickly walks to the wall, where the protective gear is hanging; he grabs a pair of heavy rubber gloves and struggles into them.

                        KEN
            We can't produce another batch of this isotope
            in the time left us - - This is our last chance.
            I don't want to lose out now!

28   C.U. JAN.

The strain is showing on his face; little beads of sweat are forming on his forehead; he runs his tongue over dry lips.

                        JAN
            Let me go. If anything happens to you the whole
            project may fail.

29   INT. LAB. MED. SHOT

                        KEN
            No, Jan. If you let go for a fraction of a
            second, the bottle will crash.

> JAN
> But--the radiation----it's deadly in there!

KEN is tying a leaded rubber apron around himself.

> KEN
> I'll protect myself - - -

> JAN (Pleading)
> This is a new--an unknown isotope, Ken!
> We don't know its effects - - -

> KEN
> Can't be helped - - - - -

> JAN
> At least get some proper protective gear.

> KEN
> There's no time - - -

KEN reaches for a pair of the protective goggles; puts them on.

> JAN
> That's not enough protection.   Too hot - - -

> KEN
> I won't be exposed for long.

> JAN
> We don't know about these rays, Ken., They
> might penetrate. Don't take the chance!

KEN grags a small portable shield.

> KEN (Quietly)
> And who'll clean up after us - when the
> bottle does fall?

JAN is silent.

> KEN
> Anyway - no radiation could be strong enough to
> do any real damage through all this shielding - -
> not in a couple of seconds.

KEN walks quickly towards the door to the 'hot' area.

> JAN
> Ken! Wait! - - - - -

30   INT. HOT AREA.

SHOT across the bottle looming large in F. G. to the door in B. G.   KEN comes
in through the door; in three steps he is at the bottle; his gloved hand reaches out
and replaces the container in its guard ring; then he quickly turns, strides to the
door, and goes back behind the shielding.

31.   INT.   LAB D.   MED SHOT.

KEN comes through the doorway from the 'hot' side; he tears off his goggles;
JAN runs to him; both men are deadly serious; JAN frantically helps KEN discard
his protective gear; then he takes him by the arm and rushes him to the door.

                    JAN
          Let's go! We'll check your radiation exposure
          badge at once - - -

The two men hurry out of the lab.

32.   INT. PHOTO LAB.

It is a small photographic laboratory with the appropriate paraphenalia; a doorway
covered by a heavy drape leads into a little darkroom. Photo technician FRED
POLLACK is busy filing away some film slides in the F.G., when the door from
the corridor opens, and KEN and JAN enter in the B.G.   FRED turns around.

                    FRED
          Hi, Dr. Rindorp...Dr. Rogers....How's - - -

JAN pays him no attention; he wastes no time; he literally tears the radiation
exposure badge off KEN'S lapel and holds it out to FRED.

                    JAN (Interrupting; grimly)
          Make it fast!

FRED is startled; he takes the badge; looks searchingly at the two men; then he turns
on his heel and disappears into the darkroom.

                    FRED
          Only take a minute - - -

33.   TWO SHOT.

KEN and JAN look at each other somberly.

                    JAN
          As soon as we know, you go see Doc Stevens,

                    KEN
          It may not be necessary.

                    JAN
          Necessary or not - you go!

The two men wait in tense silence for a few moments.

34.   MED. SHOT.

Suddenly the drape to the darkroom is pushed aside; FRED stands in the doorway;
he looks shocked; he holds the badge in his hand.

                    FRED
          What happened?

JAN (Disregarding the question)
How much?

FRED
The film should be clear----It---it-------

JAN (Insistantly)
How much?

FRED
Maximum radiation dosage - way over!

He hands the badge to KEN, who takes it.

KEN
How bad is it?

FRED
Dr. Rogers -- |----|-----

JAN (Sharply)
Well!

FRED looks at the two men; he looks stricken.

~~FRED~~
~~takes the badge from his face he~~

He looks at KEN as if he is seeing a ghost. KEN ~~lifts the badge to his face; he~~ takes the badge from Fred and
looks at it.

35.   C.U. BADGE

The inscription on it reads: Dr. Kenneth Rogers
#722
- and the small square piece of photographic film below it is jet black!

KEN
Jet black! --A fatal dose! !

DISSOLVE

36.   INT. CORRIDOR.   OUTSIDE DOC STEVENS' OFFICE.   CLOSE SHOT - DOOR.

The legend on the door reads: JONATHAN STEVENS, M.D.   CAMERA PULLS BACK
and PANS OFF to a MED. SHOT of JAN. He is waiting impatiently outside the
door; obviously he has been doing so for quite a while; he looks worried and on edge.
The door opens and KEN comes out of DOC'S office; he, too, looks worried and
serious; JAN rushes up to him.

JAN
Ken! What did Doc say?

KEN (With frowning pre-occupation)
Jan...Something is very wrong...We've got
to re-check our experiments - - -

JAN
But you! What about you?

                              KEN
Doc says .... I'm alright !

                         JAN
          What!??

                         KEN
          Gave me a clean bill of health - - -

                         JAN
          Bʉʈ ĭɫʻɔʈ̵ s ĭɱʏ̶ɔʂʂ̵ĭʉ̵ʈ̵ak That's wonderful, Ken..(Bewildered).
            -                              But......
                            KEN
          I don't understand it either...Uɳɭƨʂ̵ɽ the radiation---
                    (Resolutely)   affected the badge, but not me....
          Come on, Jan...We've got work to do-----

They start down the corridor.

                         JAN
          What did Doc say?

                         KEN
          I'll tell you what's in the report -----

                                             DISSOLVE

37   INT.   DOC STEVENS' EXAMINATION ROOM.   CLOSE SHOT.
      MEDICAL EXAMINATION REPORT.

It is being held in the hands of DR. HARRY WARNER. DR. WARNER
Director of the Karrington Atomic Research Laboratories, is a distinguished looking
man in his late fifties; he is at present ill at ease; he looks worried and harrassed.
KEN'S name appears on the report - and the black film strip from his exposure badge
is clipped on to it.
DR. WARNER lowers the report to reveal DOC STEVENS; DOC is in his early
fifties; under his gruff exterior is a man of real warmth and understanding; at the
moment he is angry and exasperated.
DOC'S Examination Room is light and airy, and has that typical asceptic look of all
places medical; it contains various cabinets with instruments and medicines; and
several intricate pieces of equipment for special examinations pertaining to radiation
disorders.

                         WARNER
          ....and you can find nothing wrong with him.....

                         DOC
          Absolutely nothing!

                         WARNER
          Then there's no problem - - -

                         DOC
          On the contrary....It's too fantastic! I've got to
          know as much as possible about that isotope...It's
          properties...Radiation intensity...Rate of disinte-
          gration...You've got to tell me...Or how can I
          know what counter measures to take? - -.-

                    WARNER
You place me in a very awkward position, Doc - - -

                    DOC (Outraged)
Awkward! Look, Harry, a man's life is at stake!

He throws the report on his desk in disgusted anger.

                    WARNER
I realize that...But this involves questions of
national security - - -

                    DOC
You're the director of this madhouse, aren't you?

                    WARNER
My hands are tied....Ken and Jan Rindorp are
working on the Army's most important project...

DOC grunts.

                    WARNER (continuing)
...The Pentagon has clamped a 'Top Secret'
classification on it...

                    DOC
I don't think you realize quite what's happened to
Ken...By every medical criterion - he should be
dead!

WARNER reacts with a startled look; DOC goes to his desk, picks up KEN'S
report again, during:

                    DOC
According to this report, Ken received an immediate
dose of hard radiation in excess of 700 roentgens
of - hmmm - 'modified' gamma rays - - -

        (He looks full at WARNER)
That's twenty times the normal radiation dosage
for a life time!

        (He waves the record at WARNER for emphasis)

He's had twice the amount of radiation that the
people of Hiroshima got! How many of them lived!?
I've given Ken every test I can think of - and I
can find nothing at all wrong with him! - - -

                    WARNER
Then maybe the radiation had no effects - - -

                    DOC (Exploding)
Hang it all, Harry! How do we know? How can I

(DOC, continuing)
even approach the problem, when I know nothing -
absolutely nothing - about what kind of cockeyed
radiation hit him! - - -

WARNER
Doc, I - - -

DOC
At least you can call the Pentagon - got permission
from some brass hat to give me the information
I need - - -

WARNER
It would be useless, Doc . . . There're no exceptions---

DOC
Blasted red tape! . . . If Ken should die . . . I'll
never forgive myself.

WARNER (Making up his mind)
Alright, Doc . . . Ken is working on Project AR-79 . . . I

DOC
Numbers mean nothing to me . . .

DOC looks alertly at WARNER.

WARNER
Then listen! Ken is developing a new, super-power fuel for
'Project Moon Race" . . . . The element he has
evolved is not a true isotope . . . rather it is . . . .

DOC has picked up a pencil and is taking notes as we:

FADE SOUND AND DISSOLVE

38   EXT. DAY. L.S. HELEN'S HOUSE.

It is noon on the suburban street.

DISSOLVE

39   INT. DAY. HELEN'S KITCHEN-DINETTE.   MED. SHOT.

It is the kitchen-dining area of a comfortable suburban home; light and airy the
windows face a back garden; there is a door (practical) leading to the basement,
and another opening out into the garden; it is neat and tastefully furnished.
KEN and his fiancee, HELEN TAYLOR, are sitting at the table finishing their
lunch. HELEN is a lovely young woman in her middle twenties; she has a warm
and friendly personality.

KEN
Darling . . . your lunch was a masterpiece . . .
Beats the lab cafeteria by a mile!

HELEN
I should hope so! - - -

                    KEN
Just don't let the quality slide down to the
baloney-and-cheese-lunchbox level after the wedding.

                    HELEN
I always cook better for a husband than for a fiancee.

            KEN (With a raised eyebrow)
Always?!

                    HELEN
In my series of one case!

KEN pulls her over to him affectionately.

                    KEN
There might not even be one case - after I get
through telling you the bad news. . .

            HELEN (Holding him at arm's length)
Ken Rogers! Don't tell me you're breaking our
date tonight!

                    KEN
You must be a mind-reader!

            HELEN (Disappointed)
Oh, Ken...Again!.....

                    KEN
I'm sorry, darling...It can't be helped...There're
some new developments...I'll have to work late...
Sorry....would you give me the keys to the Venice
Beach House...There're some books I'd like to pick
up....Really, I'm sorry.

HELEN gets up; goes to the cupboard; opens it during:

                    HELEN
Alright...I'll let you get away with it this time...
But you'd better reform the minute we leave the
Wayfarer's Chapel...or my series of one case might
grow into - two dozen!

KEN laughs; HELEN takes a small bunch of keys from a shelf in the cupboard,
turns and holds them up.

                    HELEN
Here...Catch!...

She throws the keys to KEN, who catches them, but lets them fall on the floor
during:

                    HELEN
Mother and I enjoyed our Sunday very much...too
bad you couldn't be with us...

40 C.U. KEYS ON FLOOR

It is a small bunch of keys with a large tag, plainly seen, which reads: BEACH HOUSE.
(NOTE:: It is important to establish these keys for later scene)
KEN'S hand comes into the picture as he bends down and picks up the keys, during:

KEN
I just couldn't get away.....

41 WIDER TWO SHOT

HELEN is putting some plates in the cupboard; KEN is straightening up with the keys,
putting them in his pocket....Suddenly he frowns....

HELEN
42 CLOSE SHOT. KEN   I know.

He is frowning; he passes a hand in front of his eyes; then looks tensely towards HELEN.

43 ANGLE ON HELEN. KEN'S p.o.v.

HELEN is putting the plates in the cupboard; she is humming softly; the picture seems
to waver slightly; suddenly it slowly begins to split into two seperate pictures; for a
moment everything is doubled; then it draws together again to a single picture.
HELEN has turned around; she is looking at KEN (CAMERA) with concern.

44 CLOSER ANGLE. HELEN

HELEN (Concerned)
What's the matter, Ken?

She walks over to him during:

HELEN
Anything wrong?

KEN
Wrong? No, no....Nothing's wrong...

Absentmindedly KEN touches his temple.

HELEN
Do you have a headache?

KEN
Headache?. . .

45 CLOSE SHOT. KEN.

KEN
....Why...No.....

But Ken is reminded of the accident in the lab, and the radiation with its
as yet unknown consequences. He grows momentarily sober and thoughtful.

46 CLOSE SHOT. HELEN

She regards KEN closely.

> HELEN
> Darling, there is something bothering you...not
> just a headache....What is it? You can't fool me...
> I have Extrasensory Perception...

47 TWO SHOT

> KEN
> Oh-oh...I'm glad you told me. I'm not going to
> marry a woman who can read my mind!

> HELEN
> We women know what's in a man's mind...without
> telepathic powers!

KEN suddenly realizes that he may be giving away his secret fears to HELEN;
deliberately he changes the subject.

> KEN
> You know, Helen, I used to be very interested in
> that field - back in High School in San Francisco...
> It's a fascinating subject...The Science of Para-
> psychology...telepathy...telekinesis...There's a
> lot of work to be done in that area...Sometimes I'm
> sorry I was so completely sidetracked into nuclear
> physics...The study of man's mind is just as much
> a new frontier as atomic energy...

> HELEN
> Ken...

But KEN won't be interrupted...And HELEN, knowing perfectly well that he's
trying not to talk about something - by talking a blue streak about something entirely
irrelevant - settles down to listen patiently - during:

> KEN
> You know - maybe there is a connection between
> atomic radiation - and our brain waves -- A person's
> individual mind waves might well be influenced by
> cosmic radiation - or atomic radiation waves, if you
> will...It could explain everything - from telepathy
> to ..deja vue - that strange feeling that you've been
> someplace before, but you know you never have...Or
> that something has happened exactly the same once
> already....

> HELEN
> Darling...

KEN is getting carried away with the subject; he gets up; gestures - during:

> KEN
> Atomic waves might even influence the waves radiated
> by matter itself...something's got to explain the
> inexplicable...and some fantastic things have happened...

(Continued)

(continued)
Right here in this state, for instance.....not so many years back, when thousands of big stones fell from a clear sky for weeks on somebody's house...Naither the police nor investigating scientists could explain it... Suppose that was atomic radiation waves...causing a coalescence of minute dust particles..forming those stones

48 C.U. HELEN

                    HELEN
          Lot's of strange things happen in the world.....

49 TWO SHOT - OVERLAPPING

                    HELEN
          ...Why must everything have a scientific explanation?

                    KEN
          Everything does...Only we don't as yet know all the
          explanations...There's nothing supernatural....Once
          man thought lightening was supernatural...until he
          discovered electricity! There must be some connection
          between atomic waves - and these strange phenomena...
          there must!....

KEN has run down; he stops. He looks at HELEN, who regards him with affectionate and amused tolerance.

50 C.U. HELEN

                    HELEN (Quietly)
          Alright, darling, now tell me what's really on your
          mind!

51 TWO SHOT - OVERLAPPING

                    KEN
          Can't fool you one little bit, can I?

                    HELEN (Lovingly)
          Uh-uh...I know you too well, darling...

52 C.U. KEN

For a brief moment his forehead furrows in a frown as his thoughts again go to the accident; then he deliberately erases it from his mind.

                    KEN
          Well - It's just that I'm a little disappointed with
          the progress of my work...Our last experiment threw
          us behind schedule...That's why I have to work late
          tonight...But I'll make it up to you...

KEN pulls HELEN down on his lap and kisses her; then he gives her an affectionate pat and gets up.

                    KEN
          I've got to get back to the lab....

KEN
(Continued)   (He starts away; stops)

Look, darling, I'll tell you what I'll do...I'll pick
you up at six, and we'll have dinner together...I
can be back at the lab by eight...

HELEN
You're a darling.....

DISSOLVE

53-55   INT. DAY. DOC STEVENS' EXAMINATION ROOM. CLOSE SHOT – DOC.
PULL BACK AND REVEAL KEN.

DOC (Seriously)
It's impossible! I can't find a thing wrong with you.
That momentary double vision you experienced was
probably due to strain...and you'd been bending
down...Happens to all of us...No, Ken, as far as
I can make out, you're disgustingly healthy!

KEN (Dispiritedly)
I feel fine now.....

DOC
And you've had no itching – nausea..no dry or
'dusty' feeling...no headache or chills?

KEN
No - nothing - - -

He frowns with incongruous disappointment; He is getting dressed during:

DOC (He looks at Ken curiously)
What's the matter?

KEN (With a flat voice)
Tell me, Doc, if the radiation I've been experimenting
with had potency, there should be something wrong
with me, shouldn't there?

DOC (Drily)
I'll say....Look, Ken, you're just a couple of
years over thirty....

KEN
Thirty-four - - -

DOC
Right. The radiation limit you should have
received by now..should amount to about twelve
roentgens. You've just added 700 to that...and
as far as I can determine you might as well have
been exposed to a bowl of soup as to that concoction
of yours!

                    KEN
Then my experiment is a failure! Of course.
I'm grateful I'm alive, but--it isn't easy to
face failure, after all the thought I put into
this! I don't know what the answer is....we're
re-checking every step of our process - - -

                    DOC
Just be careful in the future - Remember,
you're not conducting a high school experiment
in chemistry!

KEN grins. He has finished dressing.

                    DOC
Now get out of here -- Take it easy the rest
of the day - - -

                    KEN
You're the doctor! I'll just go down and tell Jan.

He starts to leave; DOC calls after him:

                    DOC
Same time here tomorrow.

                    KEN
Alright, Doc.

He closes the door behind him.

56   C.U. DOC

He looks after KEN with a frown of puzzlement.

57   INT. DAY. MED. SHOT. DOLLY SHOT. BUILDING Q CORRIDOR.

The corridor is empty. KEN comes around the corner; he looks serious - preoccupied. He walks to a MCU - and the CAMERA DOLLIES BACK with him as he walks down the corridor. Faintly, at first, we hear his stream-of-consciousness as the thoughts whirl through KEN'S mind. (Note: Possibly use super impositions of faces.)

                    VOICES OVER
            (Echo and reverberation chamber)

        KEN: ....my experiment is a failure...failure....

        DOC: ...you're not conducting a high school experiment . . . . .

        HELEN. . . lot's of strange things happen in the world.

        KEN . . . failure -- failure . . .

        DOC: High school experiment....high school - - -

        HELEN: Lot's of strange things....strange things---

The stream-of-consciousness becomes more urgent; KEN'S face begins to look strained.

                    VOICES OVER
        Doc: High school experiment....high school .. ..high school ....

KEN has reached the door to Experimental Lab D. He suddenly stops; he sways, reels - and begins to fall ---

58   SHOT p.o.v. KEN.

The white walls of the corridor seem to wave in and out in dizzying rhythm; the floor heaves and buckles; the lights in the ceiling above whirl and twist - as KEN staggers - and falls - to a quick . . .

                                        BLACK OUT

FADE IN:

59   INT. DAY. HIGH SCHOOL CORRIDOR. SHOT. p.o.v. KEN.

Slowly things come back into focus; KEN is staring up at the white ceiling of the corridor; he sits up on the floor.

60   WIDE SHOT.

KEN is sitting on the floor; he looks around; he shakes his head to clear it. He is in the corridor - outside the door. But the corridor looks different; the paint is old and dirty; the legend across the lab doors is gone; the frosted glass windows are painted over; the light fixtures in the ceiling look different.... and from inside the 'lab' comes a series of muffled, irregular bumps . . .

61   CLOSE SHOT.

Puzzled - and a little frightened - KEN gets up, and pushes the doors to his "Lab" open. He reacts with startled disbelief.

62   INT. DAY. GYM HALL. L.S. p.o.v. KEN.

The large gym hall is empty except for a lone boy at the far end practising his handball aim - bouncing the ball against the back guard.

63   INT. DAY. HIGH SCHOOL CORRIDOR.   MED. SHOT.

KEN is utterly baffled; he lets the doors swing shut; stands for a second in frightened indecision. He takes his forehead in his hands - and then he begins walking with increasing pace down the empty corridor.

64   ANOTHER ANGLE.

KEN is walking rapidly down the corridor; panic is beginning to take hold of him. He comes to an open door leading into a small office; he hesitates a second - then enters.

65   INT. DAY. SCHOOL OFFICE. MED. SHOT.

The office is small, featuring several book cases and a large desk stacked with papers, reports, etc. Another door - also open - leads off to an adjoining office. KEN enters hurriedly - and makes straight for the desk.

66   CLOSER ANGLE.

KEN is at the desk; he seems to be looking for something; more and more frantically he rummages through the papers - pushing some of them off the desk to fall on the floor; suddenly he sees what he is looking for.

67   C.U. BOOK.

On the edge of the desk - half buried under some papers - lies a book; we can make out clearly the legend printed on the front cover: DESK CALENDAR

68   MED. SHOT

KEN grabs the book eagerly. Suddenly a gruff voice O.S. calls:

                    VOICE (O.S.)
          Hey!

69   ANOTHER ANGLE FEATURING DOOR TO ADJOINING OFFICE.

In the doorway stands a large, scowling man; he has a broom in his hand; it is the school JANITOR.

JANITOR
What are you doing here?

KEN drops the book; he backs away . . .

JANITOR (Sharply)
Who are you, Mister? What do you want?

KEN runs to the door leading to the corridor.

JANITOR
Hey! Wait! . . .Stop!

But KEN flees out the door.

70   INT. DAY.   HIGH SCHOOL CORRIDOR. MED. SHOT

KEN comes racing out the office door, down the corridor towards the exit.

JANITOR (O.S.)
Stop! ---

71   EXT. DAY. HIGH SCHOOL ENTRANCE.   M.L.S.

KEN comes racing out the door; down a few steps towards CAMERA. He stops
and looks back.

72   CLOSE SHOT. INSCRIPTION OVER ENTRANCE. p.o.v. KEN.

The inscription reads:
GOLDEN GATE HIGH SCHOOL
San Francisco

73   MED. CLOSE SHOT. KEN

He is looking at the sign – he looks aghast; he turns to run; in his face are
mirrored his feeling of near-panic. He runs towards CAMERA – and CAMERA PANS
him past and holds as he runs down the empty campus.

DISSOLVE

74   EXT. DAY. GOLDEN GATE BRIDGE. L.S. (STOCK)

75   EXT. DAY. GOLDEN GATE PARK. ESTABLISHING SHOT. (STOCK)

76   EXT. DAY. PARK BENCH NEAR PUBLIC REST HOUSE. MED SHOT.

KEN is sitting on the bench; he is alone; he has his head in his hands; he looks
off; gets up and walks towards the resthouse.

77   ANOTHER ANGLE.

KEN walks to the small outside which is a public telephone booth; he enters
the booth.

78   INT. PARK TELEPHONE BOOTH. DAY. CLOSE SHOT.

KEN is looking in the telephone book; he dials a number. A WOMAN'S VOICE answers.

                    VOICE (O.S.) (On phone filter)

4 - 7 - 2 - 5 . . .

                    KEN (On Phone)
Hello? May I speak to Dr. Maynard, please?
I used to be a patient of his several years ago,
I . . .

                    VOICE (O.S.) (On phone; filter)
I'm sorry. Dr. Maynard is no longer active.
Dr. Wolff has taken over his mpractice. Would
you like to make an appointment?

                    KEN (On Phone)
I'd like to see the doctor - right away - - -

                    VOICE (O.S.) (On phone; filter)
Is this an emergency?

                    KEN (On phone)
Yes.

                    VOICE (O.S.) (On phone; filter)
One moment, please.

KEN waits tensely; all that can be heard is his own labored breathing; then
the VOICE on the phone returns.

                    VOICE (O.S.) (On phone; filter)
Dr. Wolff will see you at once, if you'll
come right over - - -

                                        DISSOLVE

79   INT. DAY. OFFICE OF DR. TOBIAS WOLFF. CLOSE SHOT
      DR. WOLFF. PULL BACK TO MED. TWO SHOT.

The office is a typical doctor's office! DR. WOLFF is seated behind his desk;
KEN sits in a chair before him; KEN is talking; WOLFF is listening with
pursed lips and an officious manner; he's pretty much of a 'stuffed shirt'.

                    KEN (Worried)
.....there doesn't seem to be - any explanation
at all...I know it must sound insane...Dr.
Wolff, what could be wrong with me??

WOLFF rises.

                    WOLFF (Importantly)
That's what we're going to find out .. I'd
like to give you a thorough examination first...
Take your coat and shirt off, please . . .

He walks toward the door. (Continuing)   I'll be right back.

KEN gets up.

                    KEN
            Yes, doctor - - -

He begins to take his tie off; WOLFF goes through the door to his reception room;
we hear him address his nurse before he has closed the door behind him:

              .   WOLFF
            Will you get me a line in the consultation room,
            Miss Doane . . .

80   CLOSE SHOT. KEN.

As he listens:

                    WOLFF (O.S.)
            . . . I want to talk to . . .

The door clicks shut cutting off the rest. KEN reacts; slowly he goes to the desk;
looks at the telephone standing on it; he becomes apprehensive - as he pensively
removes his tie. . . His eyes are drawn towards the telephone. CAMERA DOLLIES
IN to a CLOSE SHOT of the telephone.

81   INT. DAY. WOLFF'S CONSULTATION ROOM. CLOSE SHOT. WOLFF

He is talking on the phone.

                    WOLFF (On phone)
            Dr. Warner? This is Dr. Tobias Wolff in San
            Francisco. I have in my office a young man who
            says he works for you at the Karrington Atomic
            Research Laboratories. It's rather a curious case.
            At first I thought he might be suffering from
            amnesia. . . but he is most insistent . . .

                    WARNER (O.S.) (On phone; filter)
            Just a moment, Dr. Wolff . . .

82   INT. DAY. WARNER'S OFFICE. CLOSE SHOT. WARNER

Warner is sitting at his desk; on it stands a model of a three-stage rocket;
He is talking on the phone.

                    WARNER (On Phone)

            Who is this man?

                    WOLFF (O.S.) (On phone, filter)
            He says his name is Rogers .. Kenneth Rogers.

WARNER reacts.

                    WARNER
            You must be mistaken!

83   INT. WOLFF'S CONSULTATION ROOM. CLOSE SHOT. WOLFF.
He is on the phone.

                    WARNER (O.S.) (On phone; filter)
            That's impossible!

84   INT. WOLFF'S OFFICE. SHOT ACROSS TELEPHONE TO KEN.

KEN looks troubled; he is watching the extension telephone looming large in the
F.G. - He has stopped undressing in his apprehension.

85   INT. WOLFF'S CONSULTATION ROOM. CLOSE SHOT. WOLFF.

                    WOLFF (On Phone)
            .....I'm afraid he's had a nervous
            breakdown...He told me ...

86   INT. WARNER'S OFFICE. CLOSE SHOT WARNER.
He is listening intently.

                    WOLFF (O.S.) (On phone, filter)
            ....that he has been working on some
            project....

                    WARNER (On phone; interrupting)
            Just one moment, Dr. Wolff. Is - eh - Dr.
            Rogers still in your office?

                    WOLFF (O.S.) (On phone; filter)
            Yes.

                    WARNER (On phone)
            I'd like to make sure it is Rogers ... Ask him
            what the project number is he's working on!

87   INT. WOLFF'S OFFICE. SHOT ACROSS TELEPHONE IN F.G. TO KEN AND
DOOR IN B.G.

KEN is watching the phone as if spellbound; suddenly the door opens and Dr.
Wolff sticks his head in.

                    WOLFF
            Oh, Dr. Rogers....I took the liberty of calling
            Dr. Warner....He would like to identify you
            positively....He suggests I ask you the number
            of the project you are working on?

                    KEN (Taken by surprise)
            Dr. Warner! ... Why ...   AR - 791 .....

                    WOLFF
            Thank you.

He leaves abruptly. KEN jumps up; he looks trapped; he goes to the extension
phone; reaches for it - but thinks better of it; he looks towards the door through
which DR. WOLFF disappeared.

88   INT. WARNER'S OFFICE. CLOSE SHOT. WARNER
He is listening intently.

                    WOLFF (O.S.) On phone; filter)
          According to Dr. Rogers the project number
          is AR-79.

WARNER reacts sharply.

                    WARNER (On phone, excitedly)
          Dr. Wolff! Listen carefully! Dr. Rogers is
          here! Here in the plant.   In Los Angeles . . .

89   INT. WOLFF'S CONSULTATION ROOM. CLOSE SHOT. WOLFF.
He is listening on the phone.

                    WARNER (O.S.) (On phone; filter)
          The project you mentioned is top secret.
          No one with the exception of myself, Dr.
          Rogers and two other men here, knows it
          even exists!

90   INT. WARNER'S OFFICE. CLOSE SHOT. WARNER

                    WARNER (On phone)
          The man in your office is an imposter! He
          may be ill - but he has vital - dangerous
          information! . . .

91   INT. WOLFF'S OFFICE. CLOSE SHOT. KEN.
He is staring at the telephone; suddenly he can contain himself no longer; he
grabs the phone - and listens with mounting horror:

                    WARNER (O.S.) (On phone; filter)
          .....Hold him at all costs! He may be armed -
          take no chances....give him something...use
          any excuse, but keep him there - by force,
          if necessary....I'll get the FBI....

KEN lets the telephone receiver drop; he stares at it as if he is seeing a serpent;
then he turns - and flees from the office, through the door to the reception room.

92-3   WIDER ANGLE INCLUDING DOOR TO CONNECTING OFFICE.

DR. WOLFF comes through the door; he is sporting his best professional manner.

                    WOLFF
          Now then, Dr. Rogers . . .

He suddenly realizes that the office is empty; he flies into action - runs to the
door to the reception room - throws it open, shouting:

                    WOLFF
          Stop him! ...Miss Doane - call the police...
          he mustn't get away! . . .

He runs back to the desk - grabs the phone - dials the operator in one motion.

                    WOLFF
          Hello? Hello? ...FBI...Quick! This
          is urgent! . . .

94   INT. BUS DEPOT. DAY. MED. SHOT

There is general activity. KEN comes in through the door from the street; he has
obviously been running; he is close to being frantic; he looks around; sees a
row of phone booths and runs to them - entering one of them.

95   CLOSE SHOT. KEN IN BUS DEPOT PHONE BOOTH.
     He impatiently dials the operator.

                    KEN (On phone)
          Long distance.

96   INT. DAY. HELEN'S LIVING ROOM. SHOT ACROSS TELEPHONE TO FRONT
     DOOR IN HALL IN B. G.

The room is light and pleasant; it has the atmosphere of a happy home, and is
tastefully and comfortably furnished. The telephone is ringing. The front door
opens and HELEN comes in with a big grocery bag; she sets it down; runs
to the phone; picks it up in a CLOSE SHOT.

                    HELEN
          (She's a little out of breath; on phone)

          Hello!

                    KEN (O.S.) (On phone; filter)
          Helen?

                    HELEN (On phone; brightly)
          Oh, it's you again. I just got in....Look,
          you will try to be here by six, won't you?
          T̶h̶e̶ ̶x̶b̶e̶x̶x̶x̶x̶x̶ ̶x̶x̶x̶ ̶x̶x̶x̶x̶x̶x̶ ̶x̶x̶x̶ ̶b̶x̶ ̶b̶x̶x̶d̶x̶x̶...

The door buzzer sounds.

                    HELEN (She looks towards the door)
          Oh, dear! . . . . .

97   INT. BUS DEPOT PHONE BOOTH. CLOSE SHOT. KEN.

                    KEN (On phone)
          Darling...wait...something very strange....

                    HELEN (O.S.) (On phone; filter)
          Just a second, dear. There goes the door.
          Bye-bye...be sure to be here by six....

                    KEN (On phone)
          But I can't!

98   INT.   HELEN'S LIVING ROOM.   CLOSE SHOT.   HELEN.

> HELEN (On phone)
> Can't?   Why not?

The buzzer sounds again.

> KEN (O.S.)   (On phone; filter)
> I'm in San Francisco!

> HELEN (On phone; she laughs)
> Alright, Superman, have your little joke!. . .

> KEN (O.S.)   (On phone; filter)
> But I am . . .

> HELEN (On phone; pleasant exasperation)
> Oh, Ken!. . .I just talked to you at the lab less
> than half an hour ago . . .

The buzzer sounds insistently. HELEN calls off.

> HELEN (Calling)
> Be right there!
>   (On phone)
> I've got to run now, dear. . .someone's at
> the door. . .

99   INT. BUS DEPOT PHONE BOOTH. C.U. KEN

> KEN (On phone)
> Helen! . . .

100   INT. HELEN'S LIVING ROOM.   CLOSE SHOT HELEN IN F.G. - FRONT DOOR
IN B.G.

HELEN already has the receiver halfway down.

> HELEN (Towards phone)
> See you later! . . . .

She hangs up; runs to the door.

> HELEN
> Coming! . . . .

She reaches the door; opens it. Two men stand outside.

101   CLOSER ANGLE.

The two men look noncommittal; they are both men in their thirties; well built
and well spoken; they are FBI Agents STARK and PEARCE.

> STARK
> Miss Taylor?

(Cont.)

                    HELEN
         Yes.

STARK shows HELEN his credentials.

                    STARK
         Federal Bureau of Investigation...

              (He indicates PEARCE)

         This is Agent Pearce...My name is Stark...
         May we come in?

                    HELEN (She stands aside)
         Of course.

They enter.

                    HELEN
         Anything wrong?

                    STARK
         We'd just like to ask you a few questions,
         Miss Taylor...Just a routine investigation.

                    HELEN
         I see....

                    PEARCE
         When did you last see Dr. Kenneth Rogers?

                    HELEN (Taken by surprise),
         Why-this morning. He stopped by on his way
         to the lab....
                   (Sudden alarm)
         Has anything happened?

                    STARK
         Don't be alarmed. Your fiancee is perfectly
         alright.

                    HELEN
         Then....Why....?

                    STARK
         Miss Taylor, please treat what I am about to
         tell you in absolute confidence...

                    HELEN
         Of course...

                    STARK
         We have reason to believe that someone is
         -impersonating Dr. Rogers.

                    HELEN (S tartled)
         Impersonating Ken?

STARK
Yes.

HELEN
But - whatever for?

PEARCE
We don't know yet, Miss.......It may be in
connection with his work ...

HELEN
He never talks about his work - to me....
or anyone...

PEARCE
Have you noticed anything out of the ordinary
about Dr. Rogers lately?

HELEN
No...Nothing.

STARK
Do you know anyone in San Francisco?

HELEN
Why, yes. My....
(She suddenly remembers KEN's call; she reacts)

....fiancee ..comes from San Francisco...

STARK (Alertly)
What is it, Miss Taylor?

HELEN
I was on the phone...when you came...with
Dr. Rogers...He did say something...funny.

STARK
What?

HELEN
He said that...he was in San Francisco...
But he couldn't be!

STARK goes to the telephone; hands it to HELEN.

STARK
Miss Taylor, would you call Dr. Rogers at
the plant....right now. See if he just did
call you.

HELEN (concerned; bewildered)
Yes...of course.

She dials.

                    PEARCE
         Find out when he was last in San Francisco.

HELEN nods.

                    HELEN (On phone)
         Hello?....This is Helen Taylor....May I
         speak to Dr. Rogers, please,....Thank you.

                    STARK (Covering up the mouthpiece)
         Can you make sure you are talking to your
         fiancee?

                    HELEN
         Why, yes...I think so!

                    STARK
         Do it, please.....

                    HELEN (on phone)
         Hello?....Darling?....Listen, did you call
         just now?....You didn't?I...No, the phone
         rang - and I was too late...thought maybe it
         was you....Oh, darling, when were you last
         in San Francisco?....Over a year ago...No,
         I thought it'd be nice to go up soon...

STARK motions to her; she nods.

                    HELEN (On phone)
         By the way...What was that French phrase you
         told me about at lunch?...I've been trying to
         remember...Of course...see you later..bye-bye.
                         (She hangs up)

                    STARK
         Well?

                    HELEN
         It was....Dr. Rogers.

She stares at the phone.

                    HELEN
         Then...that other call...

                    PEARCE
         We'll check and see from where it was made.

                    STARK
         Miss Taylor...We'll have to ask you not to
         mention our visit or our conversation to Dr.
         Rogers.

                    HELEN
         Byt - why? Shouldn't he know?

> STARK
> We'll keep an eye on him...But for the next
> few weeks we don't want to worry him with
> anything.
> (Significantly)
> You understand.

> HELEN
> I--think so...I'll say nothing.

> PEARCE
> And don't you worry about the imposter...
> We'll get him...Anyway, the last place
> he's likely to show up - is Los Angeles!

DISSOLVE

102   INT. DAY. BUS DEPOT. CLOSE SHOT. SIGN.

It reads: TICKETS TO LOS ANGELES

CAMERA PULLS BACK and PANS to show a small line of people in front of the ticket office window. Among them is KEN; he looks drawn and furtive. A police officer strolls by and KEN immediately tenses and stiffens with apprehension, until the officer has passed.

It is KEN's turn at the ticket window.

103   CLOSER SHOT.

KEN is at the window.

> KEN
> Los Angeles, please...one way.....

The Ticket Seller begins to make out his ticket. Behind Ken a line of buyers begins to form. Suddenly Ken freezes

104   POV KEN

A police officer is walking toward the ticket counter.

KEN

He looks trapped. Is the officer looking for him? The last thing he needs now is police involvement, investigations and delays on delays. Forgetting all about his ticket he rapidly walks away

105
106
107

MED SHOT TICKET WINDOW

Ken is walking away.

Ticket Seller leans out of the window with KEN'S ticket in his hand.

TICKET SELLER
Hey, Mister!   Your ticket!

108   CLOSE SHOT.   TICKET SELLER'S WINDOW

He looks after the disappearing KEN with a mixture of annoyance and exasperation. The next customer steps up to the window.

TICKET SELLER
(Looking after Ken)

Some people sure don't know their own minds!

DISSOLVE

109   EXT.   DUSK.   ROAD OUTSIDE TOWN.   MED SHOT.

Near a roadsign reading: LOS ANGELES, 347 MILES ~ stands KEN: he is trying to thumb a ride. After a couple of cars go by one of them stops; KEN runs up to it and opens the right hand door.

110   SHOT ACROSS DRIVER TO KEN.

The driver (MURPHY) is alone in the car; he is a middle-aged 'loud-mouth' type. KEN is opening the car door; he leans into the car.

KEN
Los Angeles?

MURPHY
Yep, but I'll be driving all night.

KEN
I like night driving.

MURPHY (Expansively)
Hop in!.....Hop in!.....

KEN gets into the car; MURPHY starts up and drives off.

111   L.S.

The car is driving along the highway

DISSOLVE

112   EXT. NIGHT. ANOTHER STRETCH OF HIGHWAY. LS.

MURPHY'S car is traveling along.

113   TRAVELING SHOT FROM INSIDE CAR.

The car is driving along; ahead on the highway is a roadhouse diner; several
signs light up the night: FINE FOODS - OPEN ALL NIGHT - ETC. -
The car turns off the highway and stops before the diner.

114   INT. CAR FRONT SEAT.   TWO SHOT.

The car is stopped in front of the diner.

> MURPHY (He stretches)
> Ah....Almost eleven thirty....I could do
> with a cup of coffee to keep me awake...
> How about you?

> KEN (He nods)
> Alright.

> MURPHY (Digging KEN in the ribs)
> Mebbe we can scare up a little action, eh?
> (He winks broadly)

They start out of the car.

115   EXT. NIGHT.   MED. SHOT.   CAR IN FRONT OF DINER.

KEN and MURPHY come out of the car, walk to the diner and enter.

116   INT. NIGHT.   DINER.   MED. SHOT FEATURING FRONT DOOR.

The place is empty except for the counterman, HANK, who is reading a paper,
when KEN and MURPHY enter, MURPHY leading the way boistrously. HANK
reluctantly puts his reading down as his two customers enter. MURPHY acts
boorish and loudmouthed.

> MURPHY (At the top of his voice)
> Up and at 'em...Bring on the Dancing girls!
> Let's get some life into this oasis!. . .

He pushes KEN down on a stool at the counter; HANK comes up.

> HANK (Sourly)
> What'll it be?

> MURPHY
> Coffee...and for my very good friend here....
> (He suddenly turns to KEN)
> ....what did you say your name was?!
> (He laughs uproariously; slaps KEN on
> the back; doesn't wait for an answer)
> He'll have the same....in another cup, of
> course!
> (He roars again)

(Continued)

                    HANK
         Two coffees - coming up . . .

He busies himself at the urn.

117   TWO SHOT.

                    MURPHY
         Yes, sir....You sure were lucky to bum me
         for a ride....This road selling job can be a
         real drag....I always pick up hitchhikers...
         keep me company on a dull night!

                    KEN (Mumbling)
         Good idea...

                    MURPHY (Scornfully)
         Too many sissies on the road nowadays, I
         always say...Afraid to pick anyone up.....
         Think they're all - public enemy number one!
         ...Not me!....I'm not afraid of anyone.

HANK places the cups before them.

                    HANK
         Cream and sugar?

                    MURPHY
         Sure! Don't wanna do the poor cow out of a
         job!
              (He roars; he points to a tray with
               donuts)
         And one of them! . . . The one with the
         smallest hole.....
              (He roars again)

HANK gets it; outside a car can be hard approaching; it stops and the car
door opens and closes, during:

                    MURPHY (He pats his bay window)
         Can't watch the calories all the time - eh?
              (He picks up the donut; breaks it; dunks it)
              (He stuffs his mouth full of soggy donut)

KEN is drinking; we hear the door to the diner open; someone enters;
KEN looks around - and starts.

118   MED. SHOT.

At the door stands a man; he is in Sheriff's uniform! He hangs his hat on a
stand near the door and ambles over to the counter to a GROUP SHOT, and
sits down. KEN seems to want to collapse upon himself - but he sits quietly
on his stool.

                    SHERIFF
          Evening, Hank...Make it black, hot and strong...
          Man, what a night this has been!

HANK is getting the SHERIFF'S coffee.

                    HANK
          Yeah? Somebody get into old man Stoner's
          chickens again?

                    SHERIFF (Importantly)
          No. Nothing like that...We've got a regular
          manhunt on our hands!

Both KEN and MURPHY are listening; MURPHY is chomping away on his do-nut;
HANK is serving the SHERIFF.

                    HANK
          Don't say!

                    SHERIFF
          We've been sewing up the countryside all around
          San Francisco . . .

                    HANK
          Somebody bust outa Alcatraz?

                    SHERIFF
          Just as bad. The F.B.I. is kicking up a storm
          over this guy.

                    HANK (Impressed)
          Yeah? What's he done?

                    SHERIFF
          That's the funny part. I don't know. But they
          sure are anxious to get him.

                    HANK
          Who is he?

                    SHERIFF
          They don't know his name...Only got his description
          ...The idiot's trying to pass himself off as a
          famous scientist....

                    HANK
          What for?

                    SHERIFF
          Who knows? But we'll find out when we nail him...
                    (He is enjoying the reflected glory)
          We figure to bottle him up in San Francisco...
          We got roadblocks on every highway...Stake-outs
          at all depots and terminals...

MURPHY is openly eavesdropping; KEN - more and more apprehensive - puts down
a coin on the counter; MURPHY notices, during:

                    HANK
          Guy'd be a sucker trying to get through a thing like that...

> SHERIFF
> Sure would.....

> HANK
> Guess you'll get him alright...

> SHERIFF
> Trouble is, we got orders to take him alive...
> That always makes it tougher....But, we'll
> get 'im!...

MURPHY pushes the coin to KEN

> MURPHY
> No - no! My treat! Anyone riding in Murphy's
> car is Murphy's guest! My car is my castle!
> (He roars; slaps KEN on the back; calls to HANK)
> What's the bad news?

> HANK
> Quarter....

MURPHY throws a quarter on the counter.

> MURPHY
> Guess we'd better get going.

HANK collects the money; KEN and MURPHY get up and walk towards the door during:

> HANK (Sourly)
> Thanks! Come again....

> (To SHERIFF)
> How do you figure this guy'll try to get
> outa the city?

CAMERA FOLLOWS KEN and MURPHY as they go through the door; the voice of the SHERIFF can be heard distinctly.

> SHERIFF (O.S.)
> He don't know about the dragnet...He might
> easily try a bus - or a train - ...

119   EXT. NIGHT. OUTSIDE DOOR TO DINER. MED TWO SHOT.

KEN and MURPHY are coming through the door; the SHERIFF'S voice carries out clearly:

> SHERIFF (O.S.)
> ...Or, most likely...he'll try to hitchhike.....

MURPHY stops dead in his tracks; he looks with sudden realization at KEN. KEN'S face is all at once distorted by a ruthless, hard sneer; without warning

(Continued)

he delivers a stunning rabbit punch to MURPHY'S neck; even as MURPHY sinks to the steps outside the door, KEN's hand is in his pocket for the car keys; and as MURPHY tumbles down the few wooden steps, KEN is already sprinting towards his car.

120   INT. NIGHT. DINER. MED. SHOT.

Both the SHERIFF and HANK look up as there is a muffled bump and a faint moan from outside, the SHERIFF at once runs to the door.

121   EXT. NIGHT. OUTSIDE DOOR TO DINER. MED. SHOT.

The SHERIFF comes running out - closely followed by HANK; MURPHY is floundering on the handrailing; he is dazed; when he sees the SHERIFF he feebly points towards his car, where KEN can be seen just getting in.

                         MURPHY
          It's....him!.....

MURPHY's car starts up - and with screeching tires turns around, and streaks off the way it came - towards San Francisco, during:

The SHERIFF pulls out his gun, and sends a bullet flying after the car.

                         SHERIFF
          Hank! Call the station! Tell 'em that
          our man's headed back towards San Francisco!

He is running towards his patrol car - and in no time he is off in screaming pursuit of the fleeing KEN.

122   EXT. NIGHT. HIGHWAY. L.S. FROM HILL OVERLOOKING HIGHWAY.

KEN's car comes speeding down the empty highway - screeching around a bend; Suddenly the headlights are turned off - and the car careens off the highway on a narrow wagon trail into a field, and disappears behind a small shed. Hardly is the car out of sight, when the SHERIFF's car - lights flashing, siren going - comes howling in pursuit; it passes by the dirt cut-off and races out of sight. As soon as the sound of the sirens has died down, KEN's car - still without lights - returns to the highway.

123   ANGLE ON HIGHWAY.

KEN's car comes onto the highway; the lights are turned on as the car takes off in the opposite direction of the SHERIFF'S car. CAMERA PANS it roaring past, and comes to rest on a road sign. It reads: LOS ANGELES 79 MILES

                                        DISSOLVE

124   INT. DAY. WARNER'S OFFICE.

Four men are present: DR. WARNER, DOC STEVENS, AGENTS STARK and PEARCE: They all look grim and worried; STARK has the floor.

                    STARK
...by the time the local police realized they'd
been tricked - following a false trail - it was
too late.

                    WARNER (With realization)
Last night...Then - he could be ....

                    STARK (Finishing for him)
....He could be anywhere in the Western
States!

                    DOC
He seems to be a pretty ruthless fellow!

                    WARNER
But who is he? What is he?.....

                    STARK
Apparently an extremely shrewd operator.

                    WARNER
But...If this 'impersonator' is a foreign agent,
why does he call attention to himself?

                    DOC
In what way?

                    WARNER
First by his visit to Dr. Wolff...Then his
call to Helen Taylor....

                    STARK
Perhaps the bewilderment his actions are causing
is part of a cunning plan....The point is, the
man must be stopped - at all costs....Especially
if he is out to sabotage the race to get the first
manned rocket to the moon...

                    WARNER
Of course...

                    STARK
Washington wants this man - alive, if possible....
But we'll take no risks...We have orders now to
shoot if necessary...

                    DOC
Does Ken know about all this yet?

                    STARK
No. Neither he nor Dr. Rindorp have been told....

                    WARNER
No need to worry them now...this is the crucial
point in their work.....

(Continued)

DOC (Registering disapproval)
Harrumph!

STARK
We're keeping an eye on him . . .

WARNER
How can you deal with a — with a 'terrorist'
like that? . . .

STARK
We must try to keep one jump ahead of him —
until the pattern becomes clearer...

WARNER (Worried)
What if he already has all the information
he wants? What if he leaves the country?

STARK
We've anticipated a move like that, Dr. Warner.
Even now the borders...every port of embarkation...
are being sealed up tight!

DISSOLVE

125   MONTAGE.   VARIOUS BORDERS AND PORTS OF EMBARKATION.

(STOCK) (Action shots if possible)

a. Police and Border Guards checking people at the border station. Identify
    CANADIAN BORDER.

b. Police and Plainclothesmen checking departing passengers from NEW YORK
    IDELWILD INTERNATIONAL AIRPORT.

c. Harbor Police checking embarking passengers. Identify NEW ORLEANS HARBOR.

d. Police and Border Guards checking people at the border station. Identify
    MEXICAN BORDER.

e. INT. DAY. POLICE RADIO ROOM (Set — used later)
    The place is functionally furnished; a couple of female Police Radio Operators
    sit at their stations in front of microphones; they are talking; on one wall is
    a large area map of Los Angeles — the name of the city being quite legible.

f. Police and Plainclothesmen checking passenger en-planing for Hawaii.
    Establish LOS ANGELES INTERNATIONAL AIRPORT.

DISSOLVE

126   EXT. DAY. CLOSE SHOT. SIGN ON STREET.

It reads: LOS ANGELES CITY LIMITS

PAN OFF TO L.S. STREET AT CITY OUTSKIRTS.

We see on the street in the distance a diner (PETE's DINER). A man (KEN) is walking into the diner.

127   INT. DAY. PETE'S DINER   MED. SHOT

KEN enters from the street; it is a typical small diner, a couple of customers sit at one end of the counter; behind the counter JOAN ROBINSON is engaged in rinsing out some cups; JOAN is in her middle twenties; good-looking in an obvious sort of way; friendly and kind-hearted behind a fascade of protective toughness. KEN - looking apprehensive, almost furtive, and mistrusting - makes his way to the counter at the empty end. JOAN - paying him scant attention - ambles over.

CAMERA DOLLIES to a TWO SHOT.

                    JOAN
            What'll it be?

                    KEN
            Coffee....black.

                    JOAN
            Okay...

She leaves to get the coffee.

128   CLOSE SHOT. KEN.

He has the look of a hunted animal about him...But there is also something hard and ruthless about his eyes and to the set of his mouth; he 'sizes up' the other customers.

129   MED. SHOT

JOAN brings him the coffee.

                    JOAN
            Anything else?

                    KEN
            No.

He drinks...Suddenly the door o.s. slams; KEN starts - spilling some of his coffee.

130   ANOTHER ANGLE. ACROSS KEN.

A man in mechanic's clothes (ART) has just entered the diner; he goes to the counter; sits down; JOAN is watching KEN with mild curiosity because of his startled reaction; KEN looks frightened; he stares at the newcomer - then tries to hide his face behind his cup - as JOAN goes to the new customer.

                    JOAN
            Hiya, Art.

                    ART
            Hi, Joan...Gimme the usual, will 'ya?

He picks up a toothpick and begins to chew on it; JOAN turns to get a piece of apple pie.

                    JOAN
          Sure.

                    ART
          What's new and exciting?

                    JOAN
          Nothing---Pretty dull around here...

                    ART
          (He points at her meaningfully with his chewed up toothpick)

          I could change that, sweetie!

                    JOAN
          I'll bet!

She puts the pie before him; looks toward KEN.

131   CLOSE SHOT. KEN.

He puts his cup down; his face is haunted; he presses his hand to his forehead.

132   CLOSE SHOT. JOAN.

She is pouring coffee for ART; she is watching KEN; she has a slight frown of concern on her face.

                    ART (O.S.)
          Lemme know when you need me, honey!

133   MED. SHOT. KEN.

His inexplicable, frightening situation is getting the better of him. In confused despair he buries his head in his arms. JOAN walks up to him, she has the coffee pot in her hand; she is concerned.

                    JOAN
          Hey! What's the matter?

KEN looks up with a start.

                    JOAN
          You sick or something?

                    KEN
          I'm alright...

JOAN looks at him appraisingly.

                    JOAN
          You don't look so good. Can I do something
          for you?

                         KEN
              Just - leave me alone . . .

134   TWO SHOT

JOAN reacts to KEN'S rebuff - then she sees how miserable he is; she softens.

                         JOAN
              Here...Let me give you some more hot coffee....

                   (She pours coffee in his cup)
              No extra charge.

KEN looks at her; he decides she does not represent a threat.

                         KEN
              Thanks.

                         JOAN
              You know...I been watching you...You really
              don't look so hot...Why don't you go see a
              doctor or something.....:

KEN stares at her; here is a small concrete suggestion.

                         KEN (Almost to himself)
              A doctor...yes...Doc!....my appointment!...

Quickly - without a word to JOAN - he gets up and walks towards the door.

                         JOAN
              Hey, mister!

135   CLOSE SHOT. JOAN.

                         JOAN
              That'll be.....

The door slams o.s.

              ....a dime!

JOAN looks in resignation after the departed KEN; she sighs - shrugs, and digs
into the pocket of her apron; comes up with a dime - and rings it up on the
cash register.

CUT Just as the bell on the register rings, TO:

136   EXT./INT. CLOSE SHOT. GAS STATION PHONE BOOTH.

KEN is on the phone; he looks tensely expectant; we CUT TO the shot just as we
hear the phone ring on the other side; a FEMALE VOICE answers.

                         VOICE (On phone; filter)
              Good morning. Karrington Atomic Research.

KEN (On phone)
Dr. Stevens, please.

VOICE (On phone; filter)
One moment.

We hear the operator making the connection; then another FEMALE VOICE answers:

VOICE (On phone; filter)
Dr. Stevens' office.

KEN (On phone)
I want to talk to Dr. Stevens. It's urgent!

VOICE (On phone; filter)
The doctor is busy with a patient right now.

KEN (On phone; desperate)
Wait! Listen! It's Dr. Rogers...Dr. Kenneth Rogers!

VOICE (On phone; filter; puzzled)
Why yes! Dr. Stevens is with Dr. Rogers! But - how did you know? .....Hello?.....Who's calling .....Hello?.....

KEN is dazed; uncaring he slowly hangs up the receiver; as if in a nightmare he turns to leave the booth.

137   EXT. DAY. GAS STATION PHONE BOOTH AREA. MED. WIDE SHOT.

KEN comes out of the phone booth; he starts down the street; he stops! ahead of him a traffic police officer is writing out a ticket for an illegally parked car; he is not aware of KEN, but KEN turns - and walks rapidly away in the opposite direction. CAMERA PANS him and holds on a FULL SHOT of a bench at a bus stop. On the back is an advertisement for MORGAN'S MORTUARY with the motto underneath: IT IS LATER THAN YOU THINK.

DISSOLVE

138   EXT. DAY. FULL SHOT. THEATRE MARQUE.

The electric letters are dead; under a huge sign proclaiming: BURLESQUE, they spell out: GIRLS - GIRLS - REAL LIVE SHOW - GIRLS - GIRLS.

CAMERA PANS DOWN under the marque to a L.S. of Main Street downtown.....
In an effort to lose himself KEN has wandered into the least desirable neighbor-hood of the city; cheap bars with partially working neon signs and constantly working B-girls; honky-tonks; flee-bag hotels - ROOMS 75¢ - BEDS 25¢ - DORMITORY; pawn shops with extra heavy wire screen guards across the display windows; all-night movies; open-front 'book stores' selling racing tips and girlie pictures...Several Main Street habituees are abroad. Among them KEN comes walking down the street; he is be-draggled - unkempt; he is hiding his hands from view; he looks completely on edge - but on Main Street nobody notices...

In the F.G. a couple of Police Officers wander into view; KEN stops in
indecision; he turns to look at the posters of a cheap all-day, all-night movie
house.

139   REVERSE ANGLE.

KEN in F.G. is looking at the posters displayed outside the movie, and the signs:
"FOUR FEATURES" - "CONTINUOUS SHOWING" - "OPEN 24 HOURS".....

In the B.G. the Police Officers start down the street towards KEN. KEN steps
up to the box office; gets his ticket - and disappears into the movie just as
the officers walk by - utterly disinterested in him.

                                                          DISSOLVE

140   EXT. NIGHT. FULL SHOT. THEATRE MARQUEE

It is the BURLESQUE THEATRE marquee - but now the neon letters flash their
seductive message on and off in garrish colors. Again CAMERA PANS DOWN to
a L.S. of the street; gaudy neon and flashing bulb signs of the cheap bars and
movies, the dance halls and burlesque theatres throw their brazen glare into the
street; we see the movie house into which KEN went earlier in the day.

141   MED. WIDE SHOT. MOVIE HOUSE FRONT.

KEN comes out; he blinks at the lights; he needs a shave; his clothes are wrinkled -
but he seems surer of himself - as if he has decided upon a course of action; he
walks briskly down the street.

142   ANOTHER ANGLE FEATURING CHEAP BAR.

KEN comes into the picture; walks into the bar.

143   INT. SAM'S BAR.   MED. SHOT.

The place is dark, dirty, dingy and deserted - except for three frowsy B-girls
sitting at the bar, and the bored bartender, SAM; a jukebox plays softly in the
background. KEN enters from the street - he heads for the telephone booth; one
of the girls, SYLVIA, slides off her stool and intercepts him; in her twenties she
might at one time have been quite pretty, but now her face looks ravaged and
unhealthy; she smiles beseechingly, with a desperate brightness, at KEN.

144   TWO SHOT.

SYLVIA seductively places her hand on KEN'S arm.

                    SYLVIA
          Hi, handsome!

Preoccupied and not used to being accosted by strange girls KEN is startled.

                    KEN
          What!?

                    SYLVIA (With a little laugh)
          Easy, honey! I only said 'HI'!

KEN sizes up the situation quickly.

                    KEN (Coldly)
     Excuse me . . . . .

He tries to get past SYLVIA.

                    SYLVIA
     You look kinda lost . . .

KEN stops; he gives her a quick glance; he is at once on the defensive.

                    KEN (Intently)
     What made you say that?

                    SYLVIA
     You're sure jumpy, Sweetie . . .

          (She steps real close to him, seductively)

     Looks like you need someone to be real nice
     to you!

                    KEN (His voice hard)
     Leave me alone!

Again he starts towards the telephone booth; SYLVIA takes his arm.

                    SYLVIA
     Aw, c'mon....How about a little drink?

KEN pushes the girl away; she stumbles against the bar.

                    KEN
     Get away from me!

SYLVIA'S face looses its put-on radiance; briefly she flares up; then her
face literally collapses.

                    SYLVIA (Spiritless)

     Drop dead . . .

She returns to her grim vigilance on the bar stool as KEN enters the phone booth.

145   CLOSE SHOT.   BAR COUNTER.

SYLVIA is on her stool; SAM, the Bartender can be seen in the B.G.; the girl
turns to him.

                    SYLVIA (Pleadingly)
     Gimme a shot, Sam...on account...please.....

SAM shakes his head wearily; SYLVIA turns back; her face is a mask of defeat,
despair and dissipation; she glares towards the phone booth.

                              SYLVIA (Muttering to herself)
          The bum . . . . .

146   INT. PHONE BOOTH.   CLOSE SHOT.

          KEN is on the phone; we hear it ringing; a man's VOICE answers.

                              VOICE (On phone; filter)
          Hello? . . . .

                         KEN (On phone)
          Jan?   Jan Rindorp?

                         JAN (On phone; filter)
          This is Jan Rindorp speaking.

                         KEN (On phone)
          Jan...This is Ken....

                         JAN (On phone, filter)
          Yes, Ken....Where are you? We've been
          worried about you.....

                         KEN (On phone)
          Listen, Jan, I've got to talk to you...about
          that accident we had -- day before yesterday...

                    (He suddenly gets a touch of panic)

          You do remember the accident?

                         JAN (On phone; filter)
          Of course.....

                         KEN (On phone; relieved)
          Look. ...Don't question my reason for asking
          you this...It's vitally important to me...

                         JAN (On phone; filter)
          What is, Ken?

                         KEN (On phone)
          When did you last see me at the plant?!

                         JAN (On phone; filter)
          Why....yesterday.....

                         KEN (On phone)
          Thank God! I was beginning to think I'd
          lost my mind.....

                         JAN (On phone; filter)
          .....yesterday afternoon, Ken, when you came
          to the lab after your examination and told me
          you were going home.....

                         KEN (On phone)
          But - I never did.....
               (Realization suddenly hits home)
          ....go in......
               (He stops in shock)

                         JAN (On phone; filter)
          Ken? What's wrong? Where are you? Why
          don't you come over here? Or go to Helen...
          she's worried, too.....

                         KEN
               (Whispers to himself in horror)
          Helen too!. . .

                         JAN (On phone; filter)
          Hello? Ken? Where are you? ......

147   INT. NIGHT. JAN'S LIVING ROOM.   MED. SHOT.

       JAN is on the phone; behind him stand two grim looking men: Agents STARK
       and PEARCE. STARK motions impatiently to JAN, who nods with a frown.

                         JAN (On phone)
          Hello?...Where are you?...Ken? ..Ken?...

148   INT. BAR PHONE BOOTH.   CLOSE SHOT.

       The booth is empty; the telephone receiver is swinging leisurely from its cord -
       abandoned; faintly we hear JAN'S voice coming from the dangling receiver.

                         JAN (On phone; filter)
          Hello?.....Ken.......

149   INT.   NIGHT.   MED. SHOT.   JAN'S LIVING ROOM.

       JAN is on the phone; he looks worried; STARK and PEARCE are standing behind him.

                         JAN (On phone)
          Ken?. . .
               (He turns to STARK)
          He isn't there...

                         STARK
          Did he hang up?

                         JAN
          Don't think so.

       STARK takes the phone from JAN; he listens for a moment.

                         STARK
          The connection is still open...we'll trace it.

He tries to disconnect - but he can't; no dialtone appears; he jiggles the phone impatiently to no avail.

> STARK
> Blast! He's calling from the same exchange as this number...I can't disconnect!
>
> (He turns to PEARCE)
>
> Get to another phone, Jim....Have the Telephone Company trace this.

> PEARCE
> Right.

He turns to leave.

> JAN
> There's a booth down in the lobby.

> PEARCE
> Fine.

He leaves.

150   TWO SHOT.

> JAN
> That was . . . .?

> STARK
> ...The imposter. Yes. We know Dr. Rogers is at his home this moment.

> JAN
> I don't understand....

> STARK
> That's why we felt we had to let you in on it, Dr. Rindorp. We knew from another call made to Dr. Stevens that the imposter might be in Los Angeles.

> JAN
> What's he doing here?

> STARK
> Frankly - this was the last place we expected him to show up . . .

> JAN
> But - what's his game?

> STARK (Seriously)
> You and Dr. Rogers are working on a top secret government project...of an urgent nature...

> JAN
> Yes. . .

                    STARK
        It could be an attempt to slow down your work...
        by creating confusion around Dr. Rogers...Or
        it might be something more serious.

                    JAN (Startled)
        More serious?!

                    STARK
        He might plan to eliminate - Dr. Rogers....and
        substitute himself!

                    JAN
        As his double!...I see...What does Ken say?

                    STARK
        He hasn't been told yet...With all due respect to
        you, we know that he is the key man on your
        project...We felt he shouldn't be - eh - distracted.

                    JAN
        But - you've got to warn him...now, the
        imposter is here...

                    STARK
        Yes...He'll have to be informed...And we'll
        see to it that he has constant police protection...

In the B.G. PEARCE sticks his head in the door.

                    PEARCE
        Sam's Bar & Grill.   Down on Main Street.

                    STARK
        Let's go!...I hope somebody down there got
        a good look at him...

He starts off.

                                        DISSOLVE

151   INT. NIGHT. SAM'S BAR. CLOSE SHOT. TELEPHONE BOOTH.

PEARCE is just hanging up the receiver left off the hook by KEN. CAMERA PANS
to the bar counter; SAM, SYLVIA and the two other B-Girls are lined up in front
of STARK; they all look sullen and a little frightened; STARK is exasperated.

                    STARK
        ...and none of you even saw the man making
        the call?

They all deny it.

                    SAM
        Look, mister...I done nothing wrong....I
        can't afford to lose my likker liscense.....

                    SYLVIA
        Pipe down, Sam...(To Stark)..You can't pin anything on me

                    SAM
         (Jerking a dirty thumb at the B-Girls)

    Them girls are just customers...I got nothin'
    to do wit' them....

                    SYLVIA
    Yeah...And it's getting late...I gotta get
    home to mother!

She starts away.   PEARCE blocks her way.

                    PEARCE (Sharply)
    Just a moment!

                    SYLVIA (Frightened; shrilly)
    You can't keep me here! Even if you are a
    Fed! I done nothin'!....I seen nothin'!

152   THREE SHOT

STARK watches SYLVIA closely

                    STARK (To PEARCE)

    She's right, Jim....Let 'er go....

            (In an undertone--just loud enough for
            SYLVIA to hear)

    Someone else'll have seen him...Funny how
    some people can talk themselves out of a
    good thing!.....

SYLVIA, who has turned to get away, hesitates; she turns back towards STARK.

                    SYLVIA (Cagey)
    Whadda ya wanna know for? About that guy?

                    STARK
    We have to find him.

                    SYLVIA
    Is there a reward if you seen him?
        (Eagerly)
    Is that it? Is there a reward?

                    STARK
    Did you see him?

                    SYLVIA
    Well...I....

STARK steps up close to the girl.

                    STARK (Sharply)
        Alright! We've played games long enough!
        I'll tell you one reward that's sure...For
        withholding information!· For aiding and
        abetting a criminal to escape! Jail!!

SYLVIA stares at him in growing terror; finally she breaks down and begins to cry.

                        SYLVIA
        Please, mister...·I don't wanna get mixed up
        in anything....I can' afford it...

                        STARK
        Then talk!

                    SYLVIA (Sobbing)
        I got a record...there's nothin' for me...
        but this...

                        STARK
        Did you see him?

                        SYLVIA
        Yes.....

STARK takes out a photograph from his pocket; he shows it to SYLVIA.

                        STARK
        Is that the man?

SYLVIA looks at the picture with tear-wet eyes.

                        SYLVIA
        Yeah...that's him!

STARK shows the photograph to PEARCE.

                    STARK (To PEARCE)

        It's....Dr. Rogers!

                    SYLVIA (In a near whisper)
        Please...don't take me in!

STARK turns to the girl.

                        STARK
        Why don't you go home?.......

SYLVIA pulls herself up; in her tear-blinded eyes burns a mixture of despair
and defiance.

                        SYLVIA
        I....can't.....

Slowly she starts back to the bar counter.

153 CLOSE SHOT   STARK

He looks after her with compassionate concern; then he looks at the photograph he holds in his hand.

154   CLOSE UP. PHOTOGRAPH
It shows a serious man: Dr. Kenneth Rogers.

155   INT. NIGHT.   POLICE RADIO ROOM (AS SCENE 125-E) MED. SHOT.

                    OPERATOR (On mike)
          All units...all units...Man impersonating
          Dr. Kenneth Rogers definitely placed in
          Los Angeles....

156   EXT. NIGHT. STREET. CLOSE SHOT MOTORCYCLE OFFICER.

The officer is parked near a corner; over the radio on his bike the OPERATOR'S VOICE can be heard:

                    OPERATOR'S VOICE
              (Over radio;   filter)

          Check all suspects answering description
          given earlier....Repeat......

The Motorcycle Officer guns his bike and roars off down the street.

                                        DISSOLVE

157   EXT. NIGHT. CLOSE SHOT. NEON SIGN

It reads: PETE'S DINER (or available sign on location; it is the sign on the diner, where KEN met the waitress, JOAN) The sign is lit; it goes out abruptly.

158   EXT. NIGHT. FULL SHOT. PETE'S DINER

The lights go out in the diner. JOAN comes out the front door - closing it behind her; she starts to walk down the street.

159   TRUCKING SHOT. MED. CLOSE SHOT. JOAN.

She is walking on the street past the diner; as she passes a little alley on the side of the building, the figure of a man suddenly steps out and blocks her way; JOAN stops and gives a little startled outcry; the man says quickly:

                    MAN
          Wait! I won't hurt you!

He steps into the light of a street lamp; it is KEN; he looks desperate.

                    KEN
          Look! You recognize me...don't you?

JOAN is regaining her composure.

                    JOAN
          Yeah...Sure I do. You're the guy that
          took sick, or something....(Only half serious)
          Hey! You owe me a dime!....

160   TWO SHOT.

                    KEN
          What?

                    JOAN
          You owe me a dime! You took off without
          paying for your coffee.....

                    KEN (Remembering)
          Oh...yes....
               (He rummages for his money; fishes out a dime;
               it's obviously his last money; he gives it to JOAN)
          Sorry.....

                    JOAN
          That's okay...I didn't really think you were
          that sort.....
               (She looks at him)
          Is that why you came back?

                    KEN
          No...Listen - eh - ?

                    JOAN
          Joan.

                    KEN
          Joan. I need your help.....

                    JOAN
          My help? You don't even know me!

                    KEN (Miserably)
          I don't know - anyone else.....

                    JOAN (Tentatively)
          What do you want?

                    KEN
          Joan...It's difficult to explain...I've got to
          have...time to think...rest...I don't know where
          to go...do you think I could...could I come
          with you?...

          JOAN backs away from him.

                    JOAN
          Are You out of your head!?

                    KEN
            Just - for a little while....

                    JOAN
            You're balmy! I sure can't take you home
            with me!

KEN looks defeated.

                    KEN
            I - suppose not....

He leans against the wall - dejected - knowing not where to turn...JOAN
watches him speculatively.

                    JOAN
            When's the last you ate something?

                    KEN
            What? I don't know...this morning...here...

                    JOAN (Appauled)
            A cup of black coffee!

                    KEN (Wearily
            I guess so...

                    JOAN (Softly; with compassion)
            You're broke....

                    KEN
            I'm...in trouble...

                    JOAN   have
            With the police? What/you done?

                    KEN
            No, Joan...it's nothing like that...I haven't
            done anything...Believe me...

JOAN looks at him for a moment.

                    JOAN
            Look...if I let you come home with me...
            I'll make you a sandwich or something...
            you leave when I say...

                    KEN
            Of course.

                    JOAN
            Promise?

                    KEN
            Promise...

> JOAN
> Okay, then...My room's just down the street...

They start to walk away.

> JOAN
> And - we keep the door open!

DISSOLVE

161   INT. NIGHT   JOAN'S ROOM.   FULL SHOT DOOR.   IT IS AJAR.

The door leads out upon a hallway; it is being held open by a straight-backed wooden chair.   CAMERA PAN OFF, across the room.   It is a typical furnished room in a rooming house; the Hollywood type bed stands in a little alcove; there is a small sink and a hotplate behind a curtain in a converted closet; and a second door leads to the bathroom.   Two windows look down upon the street; a flashing neon sign across from the rooming house rhythmically lights up the windows from outside.   CAMERA PANS ACROSS a table with the remains of a modest meal and comes to rest on a MED. SHOT of a plush sofa that's seen better days; KEN is comfortably lying back in a corner of it; he is smoking a cigarette; JOAN is clearing the dishes from the table.

> JOAN
> ...I hope you had enough to eat...You must have
> myoxxx been starved...

> KEN
> It was fine...just fine...

He's lost in thought.

> JOAN
> I'll just stack the dishes...I can do koxxthem
> tomorrow.....

> KEN (musingly; troubled)
> Joan...Have you ever had to face a problem...
> that didn't seem to have any solution?....

> JOAN
> I was out of work once..three whole months.

JOAN walks over to KEN, she sits on the edge of the sofa; CAMERA DOLLIES IN to a CLOSE SHOT.

> JOAN (Sympathetically)
> Tell me about it.

> KEN (Almost to himself)
> Tell you about it?...It seems so..impossible...
>   (He frowns)
> There must be two of us...
>
>   (He turns to Joan)
> I'm a double man...or a multiple man, Joan!

> JOAN
> Huh?

> KEN (Thinking aloud)
> Like identical twins--only to me it's happening
> thirty years after I was born!

> JOAN
> Can I do something?

> KEN (Still thinking aloud)
> I must get back to my other self...if they'll
> let me...

JOAN looks at him with concerned bewilderment.

> KEN (Continuing)
> The isotope holds the answer...Unless I can
> get to the isotope before too long...We'll die!

                    JOAN
          Don't say that, honey!

                    KEN
          I must get back!....

                    JOAN
          Honey!....

KEN suddenly becomes aware of the girl.

                    KEN (With a wistful smile)
          You don't understand what I'm talking
          about, do you?

                    JOAN
          No.....(Quickly)......But that's okay...
          You go right ahead...

                    KEN
          I'm not so sure that I know what I'm
          talking about myself.....

JOAN looks at him speculatively.

                    JOAN
          You know what?....I got an even better job
          - afterwards...

                    KEN
          What do you mean?

                    JoAN
          After I'd been three months without one,
          I mean...I got a better one than the one I
          lost...So you see - it all worked out for the
          best!

She gives him a sidelong glance.

                    JOAN (Continuing)
          Things do sometimes, you know!....

                    KEN (With a bitter laugh)
          Maybe they do....

                    JOAN
          Sure...Some day I'll get myself a job with my
          nights free - so I can go to night school...I
          don't want to be a waitress forever, you know...
          I want to do something more interresting...I'd
          like to get a job as a secretary...or a
          receptionist...or something interresting like that...

                    KEN (He's getting drowsy)
          Joan...Why did you...help me?...

                    JOAN (Guilelessly)
          You said you needed me to.....

                    KEN (Wonderingly)
          So you did...Even though you knew I was
          in trouble....

164   C.U. JOAN

                    JOAN
          Well - it's when we're in trouble we need
          help the most

165   TWO SHOT

                    KEN (His eyes are closed; mumbling)
          The philosophy of life m- served as a blue
          plate special.....

He is asleep; Joan looks at him for a moment; she takes the cigarette from his fingers; puts it out; then she tenderly brushes his hair away from his troubled forehead....

                    JOAN (Softly)
          You're a funny one, you are!...

She stands up quietly; CAMERA WIDENS. She carefully removes KEN'S shoes she places a blanket over him. Then she quietly goes to the door, moves the chair and closes the door! She turns out the light. The room is lighted by the glow from the street lamps and signs. JOAN goes to her bed; she turns down the covers - and begins to unbutton her blouse; she suddenly looks towards the sleeping KEN.

166   CLOSE SHOT. KEN.

He is asleep.

167   MED. CLOSE SHOT. JOAN.

She smiles a wistful little smile; then she takes off her blouse and begins to undress. At an appropriate moment CAMERA PANS to a FULL SHOT of the WINDOW. It is night-dark outside - only the flashing sign rhythmically lights up the window.

                                        DISSOLVE.

168   INT. DAY. JOAN'S ROOM.. FULL SHOT WINDOW

It is daylight outside. CAMERA PANS TO JOAN'S bed; it has been slept in - but it's now empty. CAMERA PANS to a FULL SHOT of KEN; he is sleeping on the couch; the closed door can be seen in the B.G. - a note hangs from the door knob. Suddenly there is a thump as something is being thrown against the door.

KEN sits up with a start – at once fully awake. At first he looks around wildly – Then he remembers; he sees that JOAN has gone – then he notices the note on the door knob. He gets up and goes to get it.

169   CLOSER ANGLE

KEN arrives at the door; he pulls off the note and reads it.

170   CLOSE O.S. SHOT   KEN TO NOTE...

KEN is holding the note in his hand.

                JOAN's VOICE
        "Good morning! Come on down to the
        diner for coffee...."

171   MED. SHOT.

KEN grins; he starts away from the door – then remembers what woke him up; he frowns – looks at the door with apprehension. Then he carefully opens the door; just outside lies a newspaper; it is folded in half ÷ the headlines can be seen. KEN starts; quickly he bends down and picks up the paper.

172   CLOSE O.S. SHOT.   KEN TO PAPER.

KEN is holding it; the headlines scream at him:

            D A N G E R O U S   M A D M A N
            L O O S E   I N   C I T Y

...and underneath: IMPERSONATING TOP PHYSICIST

Feverishly KEN turns the paper over...From the lower half of the folded front page a picture literally jumps at him: it is STARK's photograph of KEN himself. And the caption reads:

            IF YOU SEE THIS MAN CALL POLICE

Suddenly there is a small noise o.s. – KEN looks up...

173   ANOTHER ANGLE ACROSS KEN DOWN THE HALLWAY.

In the open door to another room stands a grim-faced woman; she holds a paper in her hand; she is staring at KEN. Suddenly she turns on her heel, enters her room, and slams the door behind her.

KEN – realizing that she has seen and recognized him – whirls and runs into JOAN's room...

174   INT. DAY. JOAN'S ROOM.   ANGLE ON DOOR.

KEN comes rushing into the room; he dives for his shoes; puts them on hurriedly; breaks a shoelace in his haste.

175   INT. DAY. POLICE RADIO ROOM.   MED. CLOSE SHOT. OPERATOR.

She is talking on the mike.

                              OPERATOR
                    Car 47.... car 47.....

The RADIO SPEAKER cuts in.

                         RADIO SPEAKER (DAVIS)

        47

                              OPERATOR
              Imposter suspect reported seen 2419 Elm Street.
              Investigate.

                       RADIO SPEAKER (DAVIS)
              47. Ten-four.

176   DAY. JOAN'S ROOM. MED. SHOT.

KEN has finished getting dressed; he shrugs into his jacket as he runs to the
window and peers out into the street below.

177   EXT. DAY. L.S. KEN'S P.O.V. FROM SECOND FLOOR WINDOW.
        STREET.

It is early morning – the street is near empty.

178   INT. DAY. JOAN'S ROOM.)..MED. SHOT

KEN runs from the window to the door; cautiously he looks out; seeing it empty
he runs out into the hallway – out of frame.

179   EXT. DAY. FRONT DOOR OF ROOMING HOUSE. MED. WIDE SHOT.

KEN appears in the doorway; he looks quickly up and down the street; then he
runs out; CAMERA PANS him to a L.S. DOWN THE STREET: KEN is walking
rapidly away from CAMERA. Suddenly – ahead of him – at the far end of
the street a Police Car rounds a corner and starts down towards KEN and CAMERA;
KEN sees the car; he stops; he turns and begins to run with increasing speed back
the way he came; the Police Car suddenly opens up its siren – and with red
lights flashing screams down upon the fleeing KEN – racing towards CAMERA.
As KEN reaches JOAN'S rooming house he ducks into the front door – just as
the Police Car screeches to a halt; two POLICE OFFICERS – guns drawn –
spring from the car and run towards the entrance.

180   EXT. DAY. ROOMING HOUSE BACKYARD. ANGLE ON BACK DOOR.

The place is cluttered and dirty; the door is flung open – and KEN takes a couple
of stops into the yard, and stops; frantically he looks around.

181   ANOTHER ANGLE. ACROSS KEN.

He is looking around wildly; the yard is ill kept with all kinds of debris and
refuse lying about; across from the back door – about thirty feet away – is an

eight-foot solid wooden fence; below it is an old, tumbled down brick incinerator and several rusty garbage cans, crates and boxes; the cement flooring around the area is cracked and uneven; a collection of several empty bottles stands on one of the crates.. There is a loud crash o.s. as the POLICE OFFICERS fling open the front door - and heavy FOOTSTEPS echo from the back door as the men run down the hallway towards the yard.

KEN throws a panic-stricken glance over his shoulder; he looks trapped...
Suddenly he bends down; picks up a piece of a broken chair and hurls it at the collection of old bottles standing on the crate at the far end of the yard under the fence - and at the same time he quickly ducks behind the open back door; the wood piece hits the bottles; they topple over with a loud clatter and begin to roll down the inclined cement area with considerable noise.

> VOICE (O.S.) (DAVIS)
> Hold it, buddy!

182   ANOTHER ANGLE.

The two POLICE OFFICERS - guns in hand - come racing through the back door; they see the rolling bottles across the yard under the fence.

> POLICE OFFICER (DAVIS)   (Pointing)
> That way! Over there! . . .

They run for the fence and scale it with dexterity.
As soon as they are out of sight KEN emerges from his hiding place and runs back through the door to the rooming house.

> DISSOLVE

183   DAY. INT. PETE'S DINER. MED.SHOT.

JOAN is alone in the diner; she is getting ready for her first rush of customers; She has a stack of empty pie cartons; she picks them up and makes her way to the back door leading to the alley; she opens the door and is about to put the cartons outside - when an arm suddenly reaches in from outside and roughly pulls her through the door.

184   EXT. DAY. ALLEY AT PETE'S DINER. ANGLE ON BACK DOOR.

KEN has grabbed hold of JOAN'S arm and is pulling her through the door; quickly he clamps a hand over her mouth stifling her startled cry, and with his lips close to the ear of the frightened girl he whispers ominously:

> KEN
> Don't make a sound!

185   CLOSE TWO SHOT.

KEN is holding the girl in front of him; his hand is clamped tightly over her mouth. JOAN'S eyes widen in astonishment as she recognizes KEN's voice.

> KEN
> Are you alone?

JOAN nods her head; KEN lets her head free, but holds on to her arm; she turns to him.

> KEN (Threateningly)
> Keep quiet! Don't give me away...or....

JOAN looks at him as if she is seeing him for the first time.

> JOAN
> What's the matter with you? Why should I...?

She is interrupted by the passing howl of a Police Car SIREN; her eyes widen as she listens; she stares at KEN; KEN is tense; he looks trapped and dangerous. JOAN does not speak until the SIREN has died down in the distance.

> JOAN
> Police? I.....

KEN nods grimly.

> JOAN
> But - you said....

> KEN
> (Like a cry in the wilderness)
>
> I'm not a criminal!

> JOAN (Practically)
> Come on inside...

> KEN
> Don't try anything!

JOAN looks at him earnestly.

> JOAN (Seriously)
> I sure feel sorry for you. You don't xxxxx trust anyone,
> xxxxxx, do you? Don't you know I'dxxxxxxxx have helpe
> you...if you'd only asked!
> (She turns)
> Come on...I'll hide you....

She walks into the diner; KEN follows; in the distance more SIRENS can be heard.

186 INT. DAY. PETE'S DINER. MED. SHOT.

JOAN and KEN enter; JOAN points behind the counter.

> JOAN
> Back there...There's room...Nobody'll see
> you there...

KEN gets behind the counter; he ducks out of sight; JOAN goes behind the counter and busies herself.

                          JOAN
        You can stay there for at least a couple of
        hours...After that Pete shows up...

One of the SIRENS outside comes closer; stops.

187   CLOSE SHOT. JOAN

She stands still – listening. CAMERA sinks down, under the counter, to a CLOSE
SHOT of KEN, who is crouched there. He listens tensely. The door to the **diner**
is heard opening o.s.; FOOTSTEPS come up to the counter.

                        JOAN (O.S.)

        Morning, Officer. What's all the ruckus?

                        DAVIS (O.S.)
        Morning, Miss. We're looking for someone...

188   MED. SHOT. OVERLAPPING.

OFFICER DAVIS is standing in front of the counter; JOAN is
wiping some cups behind the counter.

                          DAVIS
        ...How long have you been here?

                          JOAN
        Oh...about an hour...since seven.

DAVIS has spied a newspaper lying on the counter; he picks it up.

                          DAVIS
        Have you taken a look at your paper yet?

189   CLOSE SHOT. KEN.

Crouched under the counter between JOAN and OFFICER DAVIS he is listening
intently. There is the sound of a paper being thrown on the counter above him.

                        DAVIS (O.S.)
        Have you seen that man?

There is a moment's silence; KEN hardly dares breathe.

                        JOAN (O.S.)
        Yes!

KEN reacts; with a tremendous effort he stays still; his face gets hard and grim.

                        DAVIS (O.S.)
        When?

                        JOAN (O.S.)
        Yesterday...Yesterday morning, it was...

63.

KEN relaxes; as he listens to Joan he begins to realize that he has found a person with loyalty, trust and unselfishness...

JOAN (O.S.)
...he was in here...same time as a friend of mine...Art....

190   MED. SHOT.

DAVIS (Interrupting)
You haven't seen him since?

JOAN
No, Officer, I haven't.....

DAVIS
He's impersonating some big shot scientist - supposed to look exactly like him...

JOAN
You don't say....

DAVIS
I understand you can't possibly tell them apart -- Don't know how he did it....the guy must be a genius at make-up...

JOAN
I'll watch out for him...

She walks to the far end of the counter with some cups to place on a stack; DAVIS turns to go.

DAVIS
Okay...Thank you...

Suddenly he walks back to the counter.

DAVIS
How about a glass of water?

He sees the tap; he picks up a glass; he begins to lean over the counter.

DAVIS
I'll get it myself.....

JOAN
No!

OFFICER DAVIS stops - startled.

JOAN (Quickly)
I'll get it for you. That tap is for soda!

She gets the water for DAVIS; he drinks.

DAVIS
Thanks...If you do see that man again - call
the police...He's dangerous!

191   C.U. KEN
He has a strange expression of incredulous discovery on his grimy, unshaven face.

JOAN (O.S.)
Sure will . . .

The door slams; KEN slowly lets his head sink down in relief; above him he can
hear the rustling of paper as JOAN reads the newspaper; after a short moment
she says softly:

JOAN (O.S.)
You know...if you really are what the
paper says you are - you oughta give yourself
up!...

KEN
They'd never believe my story...Do you?

192   C.U. JOAN

JOAN
I don't understand it...But I believe you...

193   C.U. KEN
Slowly he looks up.....

DISSOLVE

194   INT. DAY. CLOSE SHOT. LEGEND ON DOOR

It reads: LOS ANGELES POLICE DEPARTMENT
                                   Radio Room

An OFFICER comes off CAMERA; opens the door and enters - revealing the Radio
Room in a L.S.   The OPERATORS are busy on the mikes; STARK and PEARCE
are standing in front of the large wall map; CAMERA dollies in on the two
agents; STARK is placing a pin on the map.

STARK
That's where he was spotted....
    (He makes a circle with his finger) (on the map)
The entire area is being cordoned off...

195   ANOTHER ANGLE. ACROSS OPERATOR IN F.G. TO STARK AND PEARCE IN B.G.

The OPERATOR is just finishing talking on the mike.

OPERATOR (On mike)
Ten -four.
    (She turns towards STARK)
Mister Stark!

STARK goes over to her, to a TWO SHOT.

                              STARK
Yes.

                           OPERATOR
I just had a report from Dr. Rogers'
protection escort....

                         STARK (On the alert)
Yes!?

                           OPERATOR
They lost him!

                             STARK
Lost him! How?

                           OPERATOR
They said... bxxxxxxxadxxxxif he deliberately
- shook them off!

196 C.U. STARK

He frowns in worried puzzlement.

                             STARK
Can you contact the officers in the vicinity
of the Rogers house...and the Taylor home?...

197 TWO SHOT

                           OPERATOR
Right away....

She begins to make the call....

                                        DISSOLVE

198   EXT. LATE DAY. FRONT DOOR OF HELEN'S HOME. MED. CLOSE SHOT.
       OFFICER McCORD is ringing the doorbell; HELEN opens the door.

                        HELEN (Pleasantly)
Officer McCord!
    (She grows suddenly serious)
Is anything wrong?

                           McCORD
Afternoon, Miss Taylor...no-nothing's wrong..
Is Dr. Rogers here?

                            HELEN
Why, no - he isn't.

                        McCORD (Obviously disappointed)
I see.....

                            HELEN
Nothing's happened to him?!

McCORD

Now, don't you worry, Miss Taylor - it's
only....he lost his police escort in a traffic
jam on the freeway...He'll show up soon.

HELEN (concerned)
He is coming over...but I didn't really
expect him till much later...

McCORD
I guess Dr. Rogers doesn't take all this too
serious.

HELEN
(With a wistful little smile)
He's embarrassed by all the fuss they make over
him...And he doesn't like being followed!

McCORD
It's for his own protection, of course...
(Helen frowns)
Don't you worry, now...We'll kinda stick around
in the neighborhood.

HELEN
Thank you...You don't think Dr. Rogers is in
any danger, do you?

McCord (With false assurance)
Of course not!

As HELEN looks after him with a small worried frown, OFFICER McCORD walks
away from the front door.

199   WIDER ANGLE.

OFFICER McCORD is walking away from the front door; in the B.G. HELEN closes
the door going inside; McCORD walks down the driveway towards CAMERA.
CAMERA DOLLIES in to meet him; passes him and holds on a MED. WIDE SHOT
of a cellar window at the ground level of the house near the rear; it is half
concealed by brush plants; it is slowly being closed - from the inside...

200   INT. DAY   HELEN'S KITCHEN-DINETTE.   MED. SHOT.

In the F.G. can be seen the door leading down to the basement; HELEN comes
from the living room; she busies herself at a cupboard. Suddenly the door from
the basement slowly and noiselessly opens; HELEN has her back to the door and
does not see the man who quietly steps into the kitchen through the door;
it is KEN! He closes the door behind him; it clicks shut. HELEN whirls around
- startled; she recognizes KEN.

HELEN
Ken!
(She sees his bedraggled appearance)
What's happened to you!?

In the same breath she realizes that this man is not the man who stopped by earlier in the day on his way to the plant; she shrinks back against the cupboard; her eyes grow large with fear; she is face to face with "the imposter"!

                    KEN
        It's been like a nightmare...Thank God
        I'm here...

He takes a step towards HELEN; again she shrinks away in fear.

                    HELEN (Frightened; deadly quiet)

        ....Where's Ken?....What have you done
        with Ken?

KEN is stunned.

                    KEN (Thunderstruck)
        Helen! What's the matter?

He moves toward her.

                    HELEN
        Stay away from me!

                    KEN
        Look! It's _me_! Ken!

                    HELEN
        I know who you are...Why do you impersonate
        him? What do you want?

                    KEN
            (His frustration is turning to anger)
        I _am_ Ken!

                    HELEN
        Is it his work you're after? His knowledge?...

                    KEN (Exasperated)
        I know all about the work...Project Moon
        Race...AR-79...everything...It's _my_ work!...

201   C.U. HELEN
       She reacts...

                    HELEN (Thoroughly frightened)
        Who...who are you?...

202   CLOSE TWO SHOT.

KEN goes up to HELEN: he takes her roughly by the shoulders; she tries to break away, but he holds her firmly; she is petrified; she gives a short cry - then with a great effort gets herself under control. She begins to humor him while desperately thinking what to do, during:

                                            (Continued)

                              KEN
                    Stop it, Helen! You're hysterical! Look at
                    me! I am Ken!

203   C.U. HELEN. OVERLAPPING.

She looks at KEN with fear-widened eyes.

                           KEN (O.S.)
                    (Just barely controlling himself)

                    It's because the way I look, isn't it?...
                    But I haven't been home for two nights...

HELEN reacts sharply.

204   TWO SHOT - OVERLAPPING

HELEN regards KEN tensely; she seems to be reaching a decision.

                              KEN
                    So many fantastic things have happened -
                    since I found myself in San Francisco.....

                           HELEN (Tonelessly)
                    Ken...It's just...just that you startled me so.

She puts her face in her hands for a second; then - without looking at KEN -
she starts for the living room....

205   INT. DUSK. HELEN'S LIVING ROOM.   MED. SHOT.

HELEN enters from the kitchen-dinette; she walks to one of the windows; stands
for a moment looking out; KEN follows her into the room.

                              KEN
                    If you only knew...It's been - horrible.....

                            HELEN
                    I...understand...

Suddenly HELEN grabs a large vase; she holds it high - ready to hurl it through
the window.

                         HELEN (Eyes blazing)
                    Now - get out!

KEN makes a move towards her; she stops him; she gives him no chance to
prove himself in her fear.

                            HELEN
                    Wait! I'm going to throw this...right through
                    the window! Take a look out there!

KEN makexxxxmovextowardxherxbxxstopxhimxxh hurries to the other window;
he looks out.

206   EXT. DUSK L.S. SUBURBAN STREET.   KEN'S P.O.V.

OFFICER McCORD and another Motorcycle Officer are parked on their bikes across the street; they are watching the house.

207   INT. DUSK. HELEN'S LIVING ROOM.   MED. SHOT.

KEN turns back towards HELEN; he is pale and bewildered.

                    KEN
        Helen.....

                    HELEN
        I can throw this before you can get to me.

                    KEN (Staggered)
        What're you doing?!

                    HELEN
        You can hurt me before the officers come in...
        it doesn't matter...at least they'll get you...
        and Ken Will be safe.....

                    KEN
        Ken.....

                    HELEN (Vehemently)
        I know what you are. You're the imposter! You
        look like Ken...but you're just a bestial copy
        of him.....

                    KEN
        No - Helen - no!

                    HELEN
        Ken has been here - all the time! He was
        not away.....

She raises the vase higher; KEN is thunderstruck.

                    KEN (Desperate)
        Please! Helen!.....I am Ken.....!

                    HELEN
        Get out of here...this minute!

KEN is defeated; he looks uncertain; it is a stalemate; he has no choice.

                    HELEN
        You can go through the back door....

Slowly KEN turns; with increasing haste he makes for the kitchen door. CAMERA DOLLIES in on Helen; she is listening tensely; there is the sound of a door closing O.S. - she relaxes; at once she turns to look out the window.

208   EXT. DUSK L.S. SUBURBAN STREET. HELEN'S P.O.V.

The street is deserted; the Police Officers have gone!

209   INT. DUSK HELEN'S LIVING ROOM. M.C.U. HELEN.

She turns; she looks thoroughly frightened; she sets down the vase; goes to the phone, and dials....

> HELEN (On phone)
> F.B.I.?...Agent Stark...Quickly, please!

DISSOLVE

210   EXT. DUSK. SUBURBAN STREET. L.S.

There is little or no traffic on the street; a couple of cars are parked at the curb; in F.G. a narrow backyard alleyway leads into the street. KEN - angry and dishevelled - comes down the alley; cautiously he makes his way to the sidewalk and looks up and down the street; no one is in sight. KEN leans up against the fence in both emotional and physical exhaustion.

211   MED. SHOT.

KEN takes out a handkerchief to wipe his face; from his pocket an object falls to the ground before him; it is the little bunch of keys to the Beach House.

212   CLOSE SHOT. KEY ON GROUND.

The tag reading: BEACH HOUSE can be plainly seen; KEN'S WRINKLED hand comes into the picture and picks up the keys. CAMERA PULLS BACK and PANS UP to a M.C.U. as KEN picks up the keys; he looks at them - suddenly he makes up his mind; he stuffs the keys back in his pocket - and peers into the street; it is empty. He takes a deep breath and starts to walk out.

213   M.L.S.

KEN comes out of the alleyway; he walks quickly to the nearest parked car; he tries the door; it is unlocked; he peers inside at the dashboard.

214   CLOSE SHOT. DASHBOARD
The key is not in the ignition.

215   MED. SHOT.

KEN pulls the hood release; he walks to the hood; opens it and begins to tinker with the wiring.

Suddenly the sound of unmuffled motors builds up in the distance; CAMERA SINKS DOWN to a SHOT ACROSS KEN in F.G. to a L.S. DOWN THE STREET: in the distance two MOTORCYCLE OFFICERS come cruising down towards KEN. KEN'S immediate reaction is to flee, but with a tremendous effort he stays where he is - as the OFFICERS bear down upon him.....

216   MED. TWO SHOT.   LEAD TRAVEL SHOT.

The two OFFICERS – one of them OFFICER McCORD – ride slowly down the street side by side; they both watch KEN.

217   M. L. S.   ACROSS CAR AND KEN DOWN STREET

The OFFICERS are almost upon KEN; KEN bends over the exposed engine fiddling with the sparkplugs; the OFFICERS watch him – grim-faced.....

                              KEN
                  (Muttering to himself; exasperated)
              Blasted sparkplugs!. . .

He yanks at the wiring. The two OFFICERS look at each other; McCORD nods ahead – and they roar off down the street. CAMERA DOLLIES IN on KEN; for a moment he hangs limply over the car – his face wet with perspiration; he is breathing heavily; then he quickly connects a couple of wires; the motor starts up; KEN slams the hood; gets in the car – and drives off.....

                                             DISSOLVE

218   EXT. NIGHT. ROAD TO BEACH:

The car stolen by KEN comes speeding down the road; it whizzes past CAMERA (CAMERA PANS it). – and races away.

219   EXT. NIGHT. ROAD ALONG BEACH.

KEN'S stolen car comes driving fast down the road.

220   INT. NIGHT. FRONT SEAT OF CAR. HEAD-ON M. C. U. KEN (R.P.)

KEN is driving along the road; the car radio is on – playing a strange, atonal, discordant piece of music; it is suddenly interrupted by the voice of an ANNOUNCER.

                        ANNOUNCER (Radio)
              We interrupt this program for a special
              police bulletin.

221   C. U. KEN
      He listens – frowning and grim-faced.

                        ANNOUNCER (Radio)
              The Police Department has issued an urgent
              request for anyone who spots a man answering
              this description to contact the department
              at once (Brief description of KEN)

222   MED. SHOT KEN.

                        ANNOUNCER (Radio)
              The subject is believed to be driving a stolen
              car, license number LGJ 633. He may be
              armed and dangerous....

KEN reaches over and clicks off the radio.

223   REVERSE ANGLE ACROSS KEN TO ROAD AHEAD.

KEN is driving fast down the road; he rounds a bend - and slams on the brakes;
there in front of him a roadblock has been thrown across the highway; a couple
of cars are stopped there - waiting to be inspected by the police. KEN at
once begins to turn around.

224   EXT. NIGHT.   ROAD ALONG BEACH.   M.L.S.

KEN's car in F.G. has just completed its turn - and begins to race back the way
it came - when two MOTORCYCLE OFFICERS, SIRENS and RED LIGHTS going -
take off from the roadblock in pursuit.

225   INT. CAR.   TRAVEL SHOT.   ACROSS KEN AHEAD TO ROAD.

The car is racing along; in the rear view mirror the flashing RED LIGHTS from
the pursuing motorcycles can be seen; the SIRENS scream their relentless wails.
The car wheels around a curve; overtakes another car with mere inches to
spare - and reaches a long stretch of straight highway. Far in the distance
ahead a blinking LIGHT can be seen... As KEN speeds nearer he sees that it
is a Police Car blocking the road.

He is boxed!

Suddenly KEN wheels his car off the main road with screeching tires - and
careens down a bumpy dirt road.

226   EXT. NIGHT.   OIL FIELD OF ABANDONED VENICE.   MED. SHOT.

KEN's car comes bouncing down the bumpy, muddy dirt road. Almost at once
it comes to a halt at the edge of a slimy-banked canal oozing with dead,
oil-slicked water; KEN jumps from the car just as the Police Car and
Motorcycles turn into the dirt road - lights flashing and sirens howling....

KEN is in old Venice - that once luxurious replica of the beautiful Italian
city built on the Pacific Coast in a near forgotten era - and long since
invaded and conquered by those irresistable monsters of the oil field:
Derricks, pumps, wheel sheds and abandoned machinery. They now rule
the muddy canals with their once-graceful Venetian bridge spans - under
which the now oily, sluggish water lies unmoving, and they lord it over the
beaten, grotesque ruins of never-completed mansions and parks... Into this
dark, forbidding, weirdly ghostlike area KEN flees - running, crawling,
sliding and climbing; the POLICE in relentless pursuit.

227   THE VENICE AREA.   THE CHASE SEQUENCE.

The chase will be routined on location. KEN desperately flees through the
fantastic place; he ducks under cracked bridges; wades through oily mud...
The underbrush rips his clothes - his hands - his face. Behind him the inexorable
sounds of pursuit follow erratically; cold flashlight beams marking the relentlessly
oncoming police hunters....
Past ragged ruins; past huge derricks and rhythmically nodding pump shafts;
past tumble-down shacks and huge abandoned drill wheels goes the chase...
And suddenly KEN finds his way barred by a high, strong barbed wire fence!

228   MED. SHOT.

KEN frantically makes a short run along the almost insurmountable obstacle; on the other side of the fence a row of delapidated wooden buildings can be seen dimly through the gloom; there is no way through the wicked-looking fence...and KEN in desperation begins to scale the murderous, sharp-spiked barrier.

229   CLOSE SHOT.

KEN is laboriously scaling the barbed-wire fence; long, naked wire spikes gouge into his hands; tear his arms and legs...but he keeps the cries of torment locked in his chest, not to give away his position to the hunters...And at last he drops to the ground on the other side - near exhaustion from pain and exertion...

230   ANOTHER ANGLE INSIDE THE FENCE

KEN drags himself to his feet; the pursuers are almost upon him; ahead of him looms the dark form of a large, wooden, run-down building; KEN runs for a paint-peeling door; he rams into it until it gives way with a dry crack - and he stumbles inside...

CAMERA PANS QUICKLY back to the fence - and there - only a few feet from where KEN climbed across a sign hangs askew. It reads:

                    D A N G E R!
            NOT OPEN TO THE PUBLIC
                KEEP   OUT !

...and out in the dark, depressing Venice area the police hunters pass by in their search....

231   INT. NIGHT. SMALL STORE ROOM.   MED. SHOT.

The place is cluttered with all sorts of junk; it is dusty and dirty; there is only little light seeping in through the broken door. KEN stands stock still - listening....Outside the sounds of the hunters fade away - all that can be heard is KEN'S own labored breathing; across from the battered down door is another door; KEN goes to it; he opens it - and goes through.

232   INT. NIGHT. HALL   MED. SHOT.

The place is completely dark - as KEN closes the door behind him; he takes a couple of steps into the silent, impenetrable gloom; he takes out his lighter - and lights it...

At once a myriad of pinpoint lights spring to life all around him; with a startled cry KEN lets the lighter fall from his hand - it clatters to the floor with an abnormally loud noise; for a second KEN is stunned; his eyes are getting used to the darkness; a little light seeps down from a dirty skylight above; KEN detects a small movement; he whirls upon it in fear - and suddenly he sees himself surrounded by moving shapes and forms; he stumbles back; all around him figures stagger and lurch grotesquely.....

(NOTE: Trick shot employing series of mirrors; possibly shot through a one-way mirror).

In rising panic KEN rushes forward towards a little pool of light...

233 ANOTHER ANGLE.

KEN rushes into the pool of light; he can see more clearly now; he finds himself staring at a row of figures – ad infinitum.....figures milling all around him... all....himself!...

234 ANOTHER ANGLE

KEN stumbles back into the shadows; he bumps hard against a large, square, box-like booth; there is a click and the brief whirr of machinery starting – and all of a sudden a booming; mocking laughter rings out to fill the dark silence; KEN whirls around.....

235 CLOSE SHOT.

KEN faces a grotesquely distorted image of himself...terror-stricken mask of panic...wild eyes...mouth open in soundless horror....he whirls again...

236 CLOSE SHOT.

Another tormented distortion of KEN'S panic-painted face it is even more horrible and frightening...and all the time the mocking laughter booms from everywhere....

237 HALL OF MIRRORS SEQUENCE

The rest of the sequence in the HALL OF MIRRORS will be routined. KEN is in panic; he whirls around and around; from countless places distorted; warped images of himself confront him, staring at him in horror; the hellish laughter rings out in mockery; the myriad misshapen replicas of himself engulf and surround him with their demoniacally deformed and misbegotten shapes... KEN's rational mind can stand no more.

238 MED. SHOT. ROW OF DISTORTION MIRRORS.

With a cry of terror-laden anguish KEN throws himself in desperation at one of the grotesque self-images...and it shatters about him in a rain of splintered glass...Huddled in the heap of broken mirror glass KEN sees that behind it there is a boarded up doorway; with his bare hands he tears the boards away... and sobbing he runs out into the night....

239 EXT. NIGHT. L.S. CLOSED-DOWN AMUSEMENT PIER.

In F.G. - from the mouth of a narrow alley between two buildings – KEN comes running onto the main drag of the deserted Pier; he turns down the boardwalk and races away from CAMERA; in the far distance the large, contortions of a roller coaster can be seen silhouetted against the sky; on the dark building directly on the alley a large sign advertises:

                          HALL OF MIRRORS
              FUN   FUN   FUN

Alone; growing ever smaller; down the deserted, night-darkened, abandoned Amusement Pier, KEN flees – from the world gone mad; from himself; and from the derisive laughter still echoing from the empty, closed-down Hall of Mirrors...

DISSOLVE

240   EXT. NIGHT. L.S.   BEACH CABIN AND GARAGE

It is a modest cabin in a beach area which is not built up. In F.G. KEN comes into view; he stops and cautiously surveys the house; it is dark and looks peacefully deserted; quickly KEN starts towards the garage.

241   ANOTHER ANGLE FEATURING GARAGE

KEN is silently approaching the front door; suddenly he stops in shock.

242   CLOSE SHOT.   GARAGE WINDOW

The shutters are closed – but they do not fit tightly; at the bottom is a wide crack – and light from inside spills out through it.

243   C.U. KEN

He looks dangerous – like a cornered rat; he has reached his wits end in this nightmare world of terror! He is through running! ...Quickly he looks around.

244   MED. SHOT
Resolutely KEN steals up to the garage; he listens for a moment at the door; then he cautiously pushes it open and enters...

245   INT. GARAGE LABORATORY. NIGHT. MED. SHOT

The place has been made into a small, private laboratory; it is lit by only one lamp in a corner; there is another door leading to a back store room, and next to it a fireplace and a small pile of wood; there are book cases and cabinets and a large table with chemical apparatus. KEN slowly makes his way to the table; he picks up some papers lying there; looks at them with wonder...

246   ANOTHER ANGLE ACROSS KEN IN F.G. TO STORE ROOM DOOR IN B.G.

KEN is examining the papers with a puzzled frown; suddenly and quietly the figure of a man appears in the dark shadows of the store room door behind KEN; the man silently bends down; unerringly his hands find a small hatchet, half hidden in the wood pile; the light gleams on the shiny blade as he brings it up; as if warned by a sixth sense KEN suddenly turns around – and the man springs upon him....

247   ANGLE

The first violent impact throws both men to the floor – and sends a large glass test tube apparatus crashing to the floor; the man is still clutching the hatchet; in the dim light we cannot see his face too clearly...

248   ANGLE

The two men roll over the broken glass a couple of times; then the stranger gets the upper hand over the exhausted KEN; straddling him, his left hand in a vise-like grip around KEN's throat, the man holds high the gleaming hatchet - ready to smash it down into KEN's face....

249   QUICK CLOSE SHOT KEN

For a fraction of a second he is petrified; staring in unbelieving shock up into the face of his attacker....

250   CLOSE SHOT. MAN. - FROM P.O.V. KEN ON THE FLOOR

Clearly seen in a streak of light the face of the other man - a fresh cut from the broken glass on his forehead oozing blood, eyes bulging in fear and exertion - it stares back at him....It is KEN's own face! KEN ROGERS is locked in mortal battle with - himself! And then the attacker in desperation brings the hatchet down in a vicious stroke...

251   M.C.U.   KEN ON FLOOR

With a tremendous effort he just manages to roll his head aside as the hatchet descends and buries itself in the floor.

252   med. SHOT.

The effort of the blow has upset the attacker's balance; the two men tumble apart; both spring to their feet - and stand facing each other in stunned silence.

(NOTE: They are exactly alike; same features - same build - same voice - in fact one man; the differences are merely in the clothes worn and in the fact that KEN is unshaven and bedraggled - while ROGERS is clean and well-groomed and has a cut on the forehead.)

253   M.C.U. ROGERS - PULL BACK

> ROGERS
> You! What are you doing here? Who are you?

> KEN
> Don't you realize.....

> ROGERS (Vehemently)
> You're trying to steal my life..my identity... my work...Why!?...Who are you??

> KEN
> I am...you!

> ROGERS
> What!?

> KEN
> The accident...The radiation....

> ROGERS (Startled)
> How - do you - know about that?

                              KEN
        You and I are both - Ken Rogers!

                            ROGERS
        That's impossible!

                              KEN
        Incredible...Incomprehensible..But - not
        impossible...We're the living proof of that!

                            ROGERS
        Nonsense!

                              KEN
        There have been other recorded cases of bi-location...

                            ROGERS
        What are you driving at?

                              KEN
        Down through history, Ken, there have been
        men, who were present in two places at the same
        time.....

                            ROGERS
        What's that got to do with us? ..It's.....

                              KEN
        Let me finish...You'll understand...You know as
        well as I because we are both the same person.
        Take Alphonsus Liguari? He was seen at the
        Pope's deathbed - at the same time he was present
        in his own monastery...And that man in Brooklyn,
        who committed a crime at the exact time he was
        sitting in trance on a vaudeville stage...That
        famous French case, where a man killed another -
        while he was behind bars in a town fifty miles
        away...and many many more documented incidents...

                            ROGERS
        I know all that...It's a lot of fantastic drivel!

                              KEN
        The only difference between those cases and us
        is that I now know the answer, and you'll see
        the truth of it when I explain.

                    ROGERS
          You're mad!

                    KEN
          No, Ken...While you've been working at the
          lab, I've been running - hunted like a wild
          animal...But - I've had time to think.

                    ROGERS
          I know I am Ken Rogers!

                    KEN
          Yes. You are.   So am I.

ROGERS starts to interrupt; KEN stops him.

                    KEN
          No, listen to me...You've got to understand...
          Do you remember fainting in the corridor of
          the lab?

                    ROGERS (Taken aback)
          Yes...But...How....?

                    KEN
          What happened when you came to?

                    ROGERS
          I went inside...talked to Jan...

                    KEN
          And I found myself in San Francisco....
          300 miles away!

ROGERS puts his fingers to his forehead, touching the cut; he looks absentmindedly at the blood on them. KEN notices the cut.

                    KEN
          You're cut....

                    ROGERS
        Never mind that...you said - the accident?....

                    KEN
        The radiation...It had no effects that Doc
        could find...

                    ROGERS
        True...

                    KEN
        ...But it did cause a unique kind of breakdown
        of every single atom in our body...a sort of
        split-in-half...in limbo....

                ROGERS (He is collecting himself)
        Go on.....

                    KEN
        The fainting spell - the fall - the blow on
        the head...

ROGERS is grimly silent; he edges over to the large table during:

                    KEN
        Don't you see? It activated this split
        instantaneously...catapulted one of the two
        identical physical entities - me - to another
        part of the space/time continuum - San Francisco...

                ROGERS (In deep thought)
        I was thinking of San Francisco when I fell....

                    KEN
        I know! That's why I landed there - atomic
        radiation waves....just like we told Helen!

ROGERS looks at him sharply. KEN makes a move towards him; suddenly
Rogers rips open a drawer in the desk behind him and whips out a gun; he
aims it directly at KEN.

                    ROGERS
        Stand where you are!

                KEN (Shocked)
        What are you doing?

                    ROGERS
        If you make a move...I'll kill you!

                    KEN
        You can't!

                    ROGERS
        You're an imposter..A saboteur...A dangerous
        madman...The police will know how to deal with you...

253
254
256   TWO SHOT.

KEN (Desperately)
You must believe me...The very atoms of our blood...our bones...our tissues...are radioactive... with a very short half-life....
Believe me, it's the radiation, Ken...Our bodies are deteriorating at an accelerated speed. . . .

ROGERS
I don't - believe you!

KEN (Vehemently)
Then look! Look at us! We look alike..... We know the same things..... ..We are one man...each with half a life to live...and most of it gone.....

KEN is desperately trying to convince ROGERS.

KEN (Continuing)
We're lost - unless we work together...the isotope holds the answer...I'm sure of it... We must get to the lab - at once.....

ROGERS looks up sharply; KEN makes a move towards him.

ROGERS
Stay where you are!

KEN
But - I just told you.....

ROGERS
I knew you'd try to get to the lab...They warned
me against you...

KEN
Ken - listen.....

ROGERS
.....I don't profess to know how you do it - what
powers you possess. Telepathy - psychokinesis -
hypnotism....It is beyond my abilities to decide.
But I do believe you're dangerous...and I can't
trust you - no matter how logical you make it all
sound...The F.B.I. will know how to deal with you!

KEN
Wait! How are you going to convince them that
you are Dr. Rogers?!....

ROGERS
With this!
          (He brings out an I.D. badge)
Special Identification Badge - for Dr. Kenneth
Rogers -- me! They gave it to me only yesterday.....

          (He gun-gestures)

.....Along with this!

He puts the badge back in his pocket; lifts the receiver off the hook.....

ROGERS
There'll be no difficulties.....

Suddenly KEN whirls around; he grabs the phone cord and yanks it out of the
wall; the phone crashes to the floor; ROGERS instinctively grabs for it; he
is off balance for a split second; KEN immediately throws himself at his
counterpart in a low tackle; the impact sends the gun flying from ROGERS' grip.....

257 ANGLE
Both men scramble for the gun...but it is KEN who wins possession of the weapon.
ROGERS to his horror sees that he has lost control of the situation; suddenly he
kicks over the lamp - plunging the room into darkness.

KEN

Ken!.....Wait!.....

But ROGERS does not wait...The cabin door is suddenly flung open – and a
shadowy figure flits through to the outside.

258   EXT. NIGHT. M.L.S. GARAGE AND BEACH HOUSE.

ROGERS comes running out the garage door and disappears around the corner
towards the front of the house.

259   INT. NIGHT. GARAGE LABORATORY. MED. SHOT.

It is dark; KEN gropes his way through the tumbled furniture to the door and
runs outside – still with gun in hand....

260   EXT. NIGHT. L.S. FRONT OF BEACH HOUSE.

In the F.G. ROGERS' car is parked. ROGERS comes running up to it; he is
just about to get into the car, when KEN comes into view in the B.G.

KEN (Calling)

Ken!.....Wait!.....Ken!.....

ROGERS pays no heed; he starts into the car.

261   MED. CLOSE SHOT. KEN.

He brings up the gun – but he cannot shoot. The sound of the car starting up
is heard o.s.

262   REVERSE ANGLE. ACROSS KEN IN F.G. TO CAR IN B.G.

The car takes off and disappears; slowly KEN lets his gun sink to his side...

DISSOLVE

263   INT. NIGHT. WARNER'S OFFICE. MED. SHOT.

WARNER and STARK stand at the desk upon which a large area plan of the entire
plant is spread out; DOC sits with HELEN, who looks worried; in front of them
stands PEARCE. There is an air of tension in the room; everyone looks grim.
CAMERA DOLLIES IN to a THREE SHOT during:

PEARCE
....and Dr. Warner received the telephone call
from Dr. Rogers about forty minutes ago....

HELEN
He's alright? Where did he call from?

PEARCE
The call apparently was made from a public booth.
He told Dr. Warner that he'd surprised the imposter
at his beach house lab.....

                    HELEN
        I remember...he wanted to go there...

                    PEARCE
        He managed to get away from him - and he's
        on his way here now...

                    DOC
        Forty minutes...He should be here soon.

                    PEARCE
        Yes. And that's why we asked you to come over,
        Miss Taylor...Since the two men are - eh -
        so remarkably alike, we thought you might make
        a positive identification...you understand?

                    HELEN
        Of course...

                    PEARCE
        Dr. Rogers seemed to think that the imposter
        might try to get inside the restricted plant area...

He looks towards the desk; CAMERA PANS OFF him to a MED. L.S. of WARNER
and STARK at the desk; they are bent over the plan; DOLLY IN during:

                    STARK
        The main gate?

                    WARNER
        The guard has been instructed to escort Dr.
        Rogers here - the moment he arrives.

                    STARK
        Good.
            (He points to the plan)
        And these other gates?

                    WARNER
        Every possible entrance to the plant is being
        guarded...and patrols are roaming the fences...

                    STARK (Looking at the plan)
        What are these broken lines criss-crossing
        the area?

                    WARNER (He looks)
        Why - I don't know.....
            (Calling)
        Doc! Do you know about this?

264   ANOTHER ANGLE
        DOC rises; goes to the desk; looks at the plan.

> DOC
> Must be the old sewer system...from the paint
> factory days...isn't used any more...

> STARK
> Paint factory?

> WARNER
> Yes...The central part of the Research Laboratories
> is actually a converted plant, manufacturing
> luminous paint....

> STARK
> And the sewer system?

> DOC
> It carried waste materials to the river.

> STARK
> Is it filled in?

> WARNER
> I....I'm not sure...

> DOC
> It isn't.

> STARK (Grimly)
> I want guards posted along the river...at every
> one of those sewer outlets! At once!

WARNER reaches for the phone.....

DISSOLVE

265   EXT. NIGHT. L.S. RIVER BED (SHOT FROM BRIDGE)

The river bed is dry; the fairly steep banks are overgrown with shrubbery; in
the F.G. a small figure of a MAN can be seen slowly searching along the
right bank.

266   MED. SHOT

The MAN - whom we cannot identify although we can see it is either ROGERS or
KEN - is searching among the shrubbery; suddenly he stiffens and ducks down;
faintly from the distance VOICES can be heard.

> VOICE (O.S.) (RALPH) (Distant)
> Okay...that's the next to the last one...
> You stay here..Chuck and me'll take the
> other one.....

The unidentifiable MAN frantically yet quietly resumes his search...In the
distance a man laughs...The sound is nearer than before...The SEARCHER
redoubles his efforts; suddenly he finds what he is looking for - a concrete
lipped hole in the river bank about three feet in diameter, overgrown with
shrubs and weeds; hurriedly the MAN crawls into the culvert. CAMERA PANS OFF

(Continued)

to see two armed GUARDS walking down the river bed towards the culvert mouth; one of them, RALPH, has a map; he shines a flashlight on it - walks up to the culvert and shines his light into it.

> RALPH
> This is it.

> CHUCK (Sourly)
> And I had to break a date with Diane....to sit in a rotten sewer!

> RALPH
> They say some guy might try to crawl through one of them things...

RALPH shines his flashlight at the sewer again.

267   ANGLE ACROSS RALPH TO CULVERT MOUTH.

The flashlight beam does not penetrate very far into the culvert; CAMERA DOLLIES in ACROSS RALPH into the sewer opening - until it finds complete darkness, during:

> RALPH (O.S.)
> Who'd ever wanna mess around in there...
> It's clogged with that phosphorus stuff from the old days....

268   INT. SEWER

Continuation of DOLLY along the sewer; it is filled with dirt and debris; we see the figure of a MAN lying prone among the rubble...Slowly - on his belly - the MAN begins to crawl into the depth of the sewer...Dust flies up to fill the air...

269   INT. NIGHT. WARNER'S OFFICE. OPEN WITH CLOSE SHOT OF AREA PLAN WITH OLD SEWER SYSTEM. PULL BACK FAST TO MED. WIDE SHOT FEATURING THE DOOR. WARNER, DOC, HELEN, STARK, and PEARCE are all present. There is a knock at the door; everyone turns towards it.

> WARNER
> Come in!

The door is opened by a GUARD and 'DR. ROGERS' steps quickly into the office and stops. CAMERA ZOOMS TO A C.U. The man looks grim; on his forehead is a long gash...It is - ROGERS.

270   ANOTHER ANGLE

The GUARD remains standing in the doorway; HELEN runs up to ROGERS.

> HELEN
> Darling!
>   (She sees his cut)
> You're hurt.....

> ROGERS
> It's not important.....

> HELEN
> I was so worried.....

> ROGERS
> I'm alright....
> (He turns to the others)
> We have no time to lose...

STARK has stepped up to ROGERS.

271   CLOSER SHOT

The GUARD can be seen standing alertly in the B.G.

> STARK (Firmly)
> Just one moment, Dr. Rogers...

ROGERS looks at him impatiently.

> ROGERS
> The imposter's on his way here!

> WARNER
> Every entrance is guarded, Ken...

> ROGERS
> He must be stopped.

> STARK
> He will be...First - may I see your
> special identification badge?

> ROGERS
> Of course.. But xxxxxxxxxxxxxx...
> I'm Ken Rogers alright, but please hurry.....

He takes out the badge and hands it to STARK

> ROGERS
> ...The man's deranged...He's armed..
> dangerous!...

272   INT.   SEWER.   CLOSE SHOT.

The man - KEN - is desperately making his way through the sewer; a fine,
pungent dust swirls in the air; it cakes his sweaty face and permeates his clothes;
it nearly blinds him, makes his eyes smart and tear - his mouth and throat burn...
Suddenly his way is barred by an iron gate.....

273   WIDER ANGLE

The iron grate barring KEN'S way is old and rusty; it finally gives way to his
desperate effort to break it loose - and collapses in a cloud of dust; a
squeeling rat jumps past KEN and disappears down the sewer, as he steadily
crawls on.....

274   C.U. KEN

His face is caked with grime and dust; his eyes are watering; he looks desperately
determined...

275   INT. NIGHT. WARNER'S OFFICE. C.U. ROGERS. PULL BACK TO MED. SHOT

ROGERS looks impatient; the gash on his forehead is prominent; he is frowning
at STARK. STARK hands the badge back to ROGERS.

> STARK
> Thank you, Sir...

> ROGERS
> Alright. Let's go!

> STARK
> Just one more thing.....(He turns to HELEN)
> Miss Taylor...

> HELEN
> Yes?

> STARK
> I want you to ask this gentleman a very personal
> question....Something which only you and your
> fiancee could possibly know.

> HELEN (A little embarrassed)
> Yes...Of course....
> (She looks seriously at ROGERS)
> Darling...In which little church did you and
> I decide to get married?

> ROGERS
> (It's the furthest thought from his mind)
> Church?

> HELEN (Troubled)
> Yes...

> ROGERS
> Oh!....The Wayfarer's Chapel!

276   C.U. HELEN

She has tears in her eyes, but any doubts are dispelled.

> HELEN
> Yes, darling...The Wayfarer's Chapel!!

277   ANOTHER ANGLE

> STARK
> Thank you, Dr. Rogers.

STARK nods to the GUARD, who leaves, closing the door; the others join ROGERS,
HELEN and STARK; they all talk at once.

> WARNER
> What happened, Ken?

> DOC
> You had a brush with the imposter?

CAMERA has pulled back to a GROUP SHOT: ROGERS, HELEN, WARNER, DOC and the two FBI AGENTS. ROGERS suddenly looks around.

>   ROGERS
>   Where's Jan?

>   WARNER
>   Over at your lab, Ken...He's finishing
>   up a test...He couldn't leave...

>   ROGERS (Urgently)
>   Quick! Let's go! If the imposter does get
>   in - that's where he'll be headed!...

>   STARK (Sharply)
>   Why?

278   C.U. ROGERS

>   ROGERS
>   To get to the isotope!

279   INT. SEWER. MED.SHOT.

KEN - crawling along the culvert - reaches a fork, where another pipe joins the main sewer; after a moment's concentration he continues on.

280   ANOTHER ANGLE

KEN reaches a few iron rungs set into the wall of a well leading up; he has reached an old manhole; quickly he climbs up the rungs; he listens for a second, then puts his shoulders to the iron cover - and shoves...The heavy lid doesn't budge!

281   EXT. NIGHT. L.S. KARRINGTON ATOMIC RESEARCH LABORATORIES ADMINISTRATION BUILDING.

A few GUARDS are in evidence; in the B.G. a couple of searchlights can be seen sweeping the plant area; a group of people come hurrying out of the Administration Building. ROGERS and STARK in the lead, followed by WARNER, DOC, HELEN and PEARCE.

282   MED. GROUP SHOT

The little party hurries towards a group of buildings; the searchlight beams can be seen plainly.

283   C.U. ROGERS.
He looks urgent as he strides along.

284   INT. SEWER. C.U. KEN
He looks despairing as he strains to move the manhole cover; his face is contorted with exertion.

285   WIDER ANGLE
Suddenly the heavy iron lid moves a little.....

286   EXT. NIGHT. OUTSIDE BUILDING. CLOSE SHOT. GROUND.

The hard-packed ground near the building wall begins to crack and move; slowly - slowly a round patch of dirt is pushed up...

287   MED. SHOT.

Slowly the dirt-covered manhole lid slides aside and a dirty, dusty KEN cautiously peers out; seeing no one - and finding his exit well in the shadow, KEN scrambles out - crouching near the wall....Suddenly one of the searchlight beams sweeps towards the building; instantly KEN falls to the ground making himself as small and inconspicuous as possible...and the strong light beam sweeps over him - and passes on.

288   CLOSER SHOT

Carefully KEN sits up - and a weird phenomenon occurs; as the darkness again closes in around him, he begins to glow whitely luminous! He looks at himself in horror.

KEN (Aghast; to himself)
The phosphorus!...

The phosphorus powder from the old culvert, which covers KEN from head to foot, has absorbed the light from the strong searchlight beam....KEN is phosphorescent - like a luminous ghost he glows in the dark! Huddled against the wall of the building he looks off anxiously.....

289   EXT. NIGHT. L.S. KEN'S P.O.V. ENTRANCE TO BUILDING Q.
No one is in sight.

290   MED. SHOT. KEN
Suddenly he jumps to his feet and races for Building Q

291   EXT. NIGHT. L.S. ACROSS TWO GUARDS IN F.G. TO THE DARK BUILDING AREA IN THE B.G.

Suddenly a luminous figure can be seen running around a corner and sprinting for the Building Q entrance.

GUARD (Startled)

Look!....It's him!.....

He quickly takes out his gun - and sends a couple of shots crashing after the glowing, fleeing figure...The other GUARD follows suit; and an alarm SIREN goes off in the near distance...and KEN tears through the entrance to Building Q.

292   INT. NIGHT. CORRIDOR OF BUILDING Q. M.L.S. FEATURING MAIN ENTRANC

KEN - face and clothing covered with dust (no longer luminous in the light) - comes running into the corridor through the main entrance; he races towards the door towards Experimental Lab D - about half way down the Hallway; CAMERA PANS him past; when the L-shaped corner at the other end of the

(Continued)

corridor comes into view, we see a group of people hurrying around the corner – also headed for lab D; in the lead are ROGERS and STARK, closely followed by WARNER, HELEN, DOC and PEARCE.

                    ROGERS (Seeing KEN)
        He's here!

He leaps forward to intercept KEN before he can get to the Lab door; STARK and the others follow; but KEN has a head start; he reaches the door ahead of ROGERS – and runs through.....

293   INT. EXPERIMENTAL LAB D. MED. SHOT. ANGLE FEATURING DOOR.

KEN comes racing into the lab. JAN is at the control panel; he turns – startled.

                    JAN
        Ken! What happened?.....

                    KEN
        Jan...there's no time...help me!...

Before JAN can answer, ROGERS comes flying into the room.

                    ROGERS
        Jan! ...Stop him!

At the same instant KEN slams the door to the corridor shut, just as STARK reaches it – and rams home a heavy iron bolt.....

                    KEN
        Now – you've got to listen..both of you!

                    ROGERS
        Jan! Let's get him!.....

JAN is completely confused; before he can take any action ROGERS leaps at KEN; the two men crash to the ground – and roll dangerously near the opening into the 'hot' area.

                    JAN (Startled)
        Ken! Watch out! The isotope's on the
        table!!

Even as he shouts his warning he runs to the control panel; slams home the switch that activates the remote control conveyor and the turntable; lights spring to life on the board...

294   CLOSE SHOT. STOCK.

The large storage bottle locked to the turntable starts to revolve towards the conveyor belt and lock.

295   MED. SHOT.

KEN and ROGERS are grimly struggling on the floor; the hammering on the door gets louder; JAN – not knowing whom to help – runs to the door – opens it...

At the same time KEN has managed to get halfway to his feet; ROGERS - with renewed fury - strikes out at him; at the exact instant STARK and the others burst into the lab - both KEN and ROGERS tumble through the opening in the concrete and lead shielding wall into the 'hot'area! STARK is about to follow - but JAN stops him.

                                JAN
              No! Not in there! Radiation!!

He runs to one of the observation ports; STARK follows suit; the others look up at the overhead mirrors...

296   ANGLE ON TWO PORTS P.O.V. 'HOT' AREA.

The horrified faces of JAN and STARK appear in the ports, staring into the area where KEN and ROGERS are fighting viciously.

297   MED. SHOT 'HOT' AREA.

KEN and ROGERS are fighting; the fight will be routined; near them the storage bottle containing the radioactive isotope has reached the conveyor belt it is starting away from the battling men.

298   CLOSE SHOT. PORT. P.O.V. 'HOT' AREA.

JAN'S shocked face is pushed aside and replaced with the face of HELEN: she looks terrified as she strains to see; suddenly her eyes open wide in dread shock, and she screams noiselessly behind the thick wall at what she sees...

299   CLOSE TWO SHOT. KEN AND ROGERS IN 'HOT' AREA.
        A startling development occurs. As the men struggle desperately, they suddenly change.
        At first only the face of Rogers, with the gash, on his forehead, can be seen
        It is the face of an old man, wrinkled and veined! In their fight, the men turn, and Ken's
        face comes into view.

300   C.U. KEN

His dusty, desperate face turns into CAMERA; showing the strain of the fight. It, too, is the withered face of an old man!

301   MED.S HOT LAB.

At the port HELEN sinks to the floor in a dead faint; DOC and PEARCE take her to a chair; WARNER steps to the port; JAN is urgently watching the control panel lights - tracing the progress of the deadly isotope away from the men.

302   MED. SHOT. 'HOT' AREA.

KEN and ROGERS are still fighting; suddenly they lurch against the conveyor belt; the isotope storage bottle is jarred from its guard - and crashes to the floor shattering on the concrete....At once a dense, seething cloud-mass of radioactive vapor shoots across the floor in a billowing explosion; almost at the same instant KEN and ROGERS fall to the floor - to become half hidden in the swirling, frothing, dense, fog-like vapor...

303   MED. SHOT. LAB.
There is feverish activity; DOC calls:

              DOC
      The ventilating fan!

JAN rushes to activate the fan operating behind the wall in the 'hot' area;
WARNER is on the phone; over the general hubbub we hear him...

           WARNER (On Phone)
    ...I want two men...in full protective gear...
    Experimental Lab D...at once!

The others are excitedly watching at the ports and in the overhead mirror;
PEARCE points to the mirror.

           PEARCE
    Warner!.....Look!...

304   CLOSE SHOT. MIRROR
In it is reflected the 'hot' area; in the dense, heavy radioactive vapor-swirl
on the concrete floor can be seen the forms of KEN and ROGERS; they are
struggling weakly; even as we watch they become almost still - and a
strange, shimmering effect envelops them...

305   MED. SHOT. 'HOT' AREA.

In the seething, shimmering vapor KEN and ROGERS lie side by side - still
now....And a fantastic sight unfolds itself before the eyes of the horrified
watchers...It is as if the very flesh dissolves from the men's bones - leaving
only the dark outlines of their skeletons...

306   C.U. STARK THROUGH PORT
His face is incredulous - aghast!

307   C.U. WARNER THROUGH PORT
He looks horrified...He cannot believe his eyes.

308   MED. SHOT. 'HOT' AREA

In the boiling, bubbling vapor pool the darkish outlines seem to merge; soon it
is apparent that there is only one man lying in the ground-heavy mist...
The atoms of KEN and ROGERS have incredibly merged; the man is whole again!
The decontamination fan behind the wall begins to have effect; slowly at first -
then more and more rapidly the lethal vapor is sucked out of the area and off
the prostrate man..until it is obvious that there is indeed only one single man -
lying motionless on the concrete floor...

309   MED. SHOT. LAB.
The people look at each other in uncomprehending shock.

           STARK (Dazed)
    Dr. Warner...what?.....

WARNER shakes his head.

WARNER
I...don't know...what to say.....

They all watch the still figure in the overhead mirror; HELEN - with DOC in attendance - begins to come around; she looks up at the mirror.

HELEN
Ken!

310   CLOSE SHOT. MIRROR.
The quiet figure of the scientist can be seen lying on the floor.

311   C.U. KEN ROGERS

His face is caked with grimy dust...and on his forehead is a deep gash! It is the face of KEN, and the face of ROGERS - merged; it is the face of DR. KENNETH ROGERS - and he looks young again!

312   MED. SHOT. LAB.
Everyone is watching the mirror as if spell-bound; the door opens and two RESCUE CREWMEN come hurrying into the room; they are both clad in full protective gear against radioactive rays and carry various small instruments; in effect they look like men from Mars, with their weird, ant-like antennae protruding from their heads, their fantastic goggles and face masks.

WARNER turns to them.

WARNER (Subdued)

In there.....

The two CREWMEN start towards the wall opening.

DISSOLVE

313   EXT. DAY. L.S. LARGE HOSPITAL BUILDING (STOCK)

314   INT. DAY. MED. SHOT. HOSPITAL ROOM

It is a typical private room in a modern hospital; in the bed sits KEN; he looks relaxed and happy; the cut on his forehead is healing. On the edge of the bed sits HELEN; on the other side stands WARNER; DOC is at the foot of the bed checking the patient chart and grunting in satisfaction during:

WARNER
...and we are all agreed that what we witnessed in your laboratory, Ken, stays with us.....

315   C.U. WARNER - OVERLAPPING

warner (expansively)
The important thing, anyway, is that Project AR-79 is an unqualified success.....

316   GROUP SHOT - OVERLAPPING

WARNER
...and that we now know its secrets are safe with us.....

                          DOC
          Come on, Harry, no speeches...
               (He looks sternly at KEN)
          And you take it easy!

                    KEN
          Sure, Doc!

          -         DOC (With a gleam in his eye)
          Tomorrow...you and I have an appointment!

                         KEN (Mock horror)
          On, no! Not again!

                    DOC
          You just wait...I've thought up a whole
          new batch of tests!

DOC and WARNER start for the door.

                    KEN
          By the way, Doc, aren't you looking for a new
          receptionist?

                    DOC
          I am...a nice, dependable girl.....

                    KEN
          I know just the girl for you...name's
          Joan.....

CAMERA DOLLIES IN TO A TWO SHOT during:

                    DOC (O.S.)
          Good.....

                    KEN
          And Doc...Fix it up so she'll get to meet
          Jan...
               (He winks; turns to Helen)
          He needs an understanding woman, too!

The door closes O.S.

                    HELEN
          Who's Joan?

                    KEN
          Someone ~ who taught my 'alter ego' the true
          meaning of understanding and kindness...

                    HELEN
          I wish I'd known more about that other Ken...

> KEN (Seriously)
> I'm not so sure you'd have liked him...or
> his impulses for violence...But I think I've
> grown as a man for knowing him so well...
> We are none of us all good or all bad...Everyone
> has to cope with - a hidden self...

> HELEN (With a little smile)
> But not quite as spectacularly!

KEN laughs; the door opens and JAN enters; KEN sees him; he sits up excitedly
and calls to him before JAN has a chance to say anything:

> KEN
> Jan! Am I glad to see you! I've been thinking
> ...do you realize the ramifications of this thing?
> We can learn to split...to multiply living atoms!
> ...Just the possibilities of regeneration alone...
> limbs...organs...whole bodies...

KEN has fired JAN with his enthusiasm; both men are carried away; HELEN sits
back with a little smile; she is used to this - she has her own scientist fiancee
back again...

> KEN (Continuing)
> We'll start on it as soon as Doc'll let me
> out of here...

> JAN
> I'll get everything ready...

> KEN
> There's so much to be done...it'll be a lot
> of work...

He suddenly becomes aware of HELEN; he turns to her - a little subdued...

> KEN (Continuing)
> Darling...You understand...You don't
> mind?

> HELEN
> No, I don't mind, dear...Just be careful...
> I don't want another accident...
>   (She smiles at him)
> You know, it's not easy to be engaged to two
> men - at the same time!

KEN takes her hand affectionately; and with his girl on one side, and his
colleague on the other he is a happy man...

> KEN
> We'll turn that accident into a real asset...

317   CAMERA DOLLIES IN to a CLOSE SHOT of KEN during:

KEN (Continuing).
....If half-life can be achieved, why not
double life?!....Think of it - a double
life span!....Only our own imaginations
limit what the future can bring!.....

FADE OUT

THE END

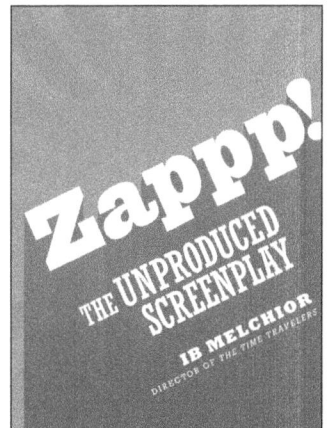

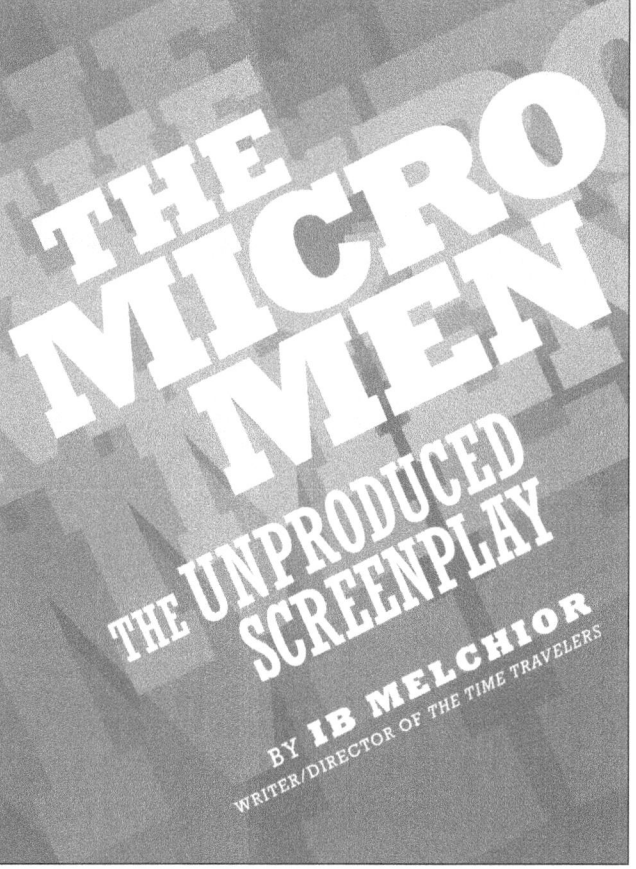